American Neurosurgeon:

The Search for the Soul

SHIVANI BINDAL

AJAY BINDAL, M.D.

DEDICATION

To all neurosurgeons, who have advanced the art and science of neurosurgery and who pioneered the advanced techniques that have saved so many lives.

SHIVANI BINDAL AND AJAY BINDAL, M.D.

The following stories are based on true events. Some names, details, and timelines have been altered to protect the identity of those involved.

SHIVANI BINDAL AND AJAY BINDAL, M.D.

CONTENTS

ACKNOWLEDGMENTS

We would like to acknowledge the patients and their families, nurses, office staff, and the American public, who have made this care possible.

PREFACE

My name is Shivani Bindal, and I am a medical student. In medical school, I've learned a lot about the human body, and I often talk to my dad, who is a physician, about all the things I learned. One day he challenged me, "Alright, so they taught you about the human body, but what have you learned about the human soul?"

I didn't have an answer. How do you find something if you don't know where it is, if you don't know what it looks like, what surrounds it, what its relationship is to everything else? How do you discover something that is not taught or spoken of?

My father is an American neurosurgeon. Neurosurgeons are physicians that specialize in the diagnosis and treatment of diseases of the brain, spinal cord, and peripheral nervous system. They operate on the brain, spine, and extremities. It is a rigorous undertaking, and it is one of the most demanding fields in medicine.

The journey of a neurosurgeon is a journey that few have ever experienced. Neurosurgeons require a special degree of physical and mental stamina that allows them to perform complex surgical procedures that can extend for hours on end. Those that choose the field are drawn to the intellectual challenge that neurosurgery offers. They must be willing to make difficult decisions that can alter the lives of patients dramatically. They are the light in the darkness. They give hope to patients who are desperate. They treat dark, devastating diseases that are poorly understood. As the daughter of a neurosurgeon, I've had the unique opportunity to have a glimpse into this journey.

Some people may crudely describe neurosurgery as the field of cracking skulls, breaking spines, and slitting throats. There is no person in history that can incur this level of violence on another human being, then have their victim thank them. Surgeons have the power to convince people to voluntarily subject themselves to what is essentially an act of violence, with the possibility of death. It is a power that very few people have. It is akin to having the ability to persuade people to jump off a cliff. You could argue a General has this power as well over his soldiers. But even a General cannot convince a civilian to jump, while a doctor can. This power that surgeons wield stems from the tremendous faith that the general public has in physicians. It is the physician's "power of persuasion", and it exists only because it is never abused.

I was born while my dad was still a neurosurgery resident (physician in training) at the Mayfield Clinic in Cincinnati, Ohio. I watched him work some of the hardest years of his life with sacrifice and commitment as he built his practice in Houston, Texas. Growing up, my father was hard on me. He demanded excellence, and he had great expectations. He raised me with the values that he believed made the best student, resident, and ultimately, the best practicing physician. He taught me to embrace "three A's" early in life: availability, affability, and ability. "Always work with a smile on your face," he would say. He taught me the importance of integrity and honesty. "Never lie to a neurosurgeon. They'll always know the truth." Though he was my greatest critic, he was always my greatest supporter.

I asked my father once, "Did you always want to be a neurosurgeon?"

"No," he told me. "I wanted to be a nuclear physicist, like your grandfather. I wanted to understand the universe. But then I went into medicine, and I decided that the best path, before trying to understand the universe, is to understand the human brain."

I later came to understand the universe as God, and the brain as the soul. I came to understand that my father's quest to understand the brain was a search for the soul. Here I share stories told to me by my father that reflect this search.

PART I
FAITH

CHAPTER ONE

Faith was hard to come by these days. Archer had spent his whole life upholding his strong Christian beliefs, yet he felt these convictions had recently been shattered. Faith, so it seemed, was a delicate thing. It easily slipped between one's fingers, leaving behind an emptiness of despair, fear and anxiety.

Thunder clapped outside. A bolt of lightning lit up the dark sky as rain fell in an endless, monotonous tone. It was as if heaven was weeping. Archer's once bright, warm home had turned cold and dark, the white painted walls obscured into shades of gray. Archer sighed as he stretched his legs slowly and painfully. He could hear his wife sobbing in the next room. He wished he could do something to comfort her in some way, but that was impossible. Now, he looked inwards. He sought the guidance of his Lord to revitalize the beliefs he once had. "This can't be it," Archer thought to himself. "This isn't the end. I know it isn't."

Archer's son, Bryan, bustled into the room. He set down the medical journals and textbooks piled high in his arms. "Dad, where's the phone? I need to make another call," said Archer's son. His stressed voice quivered with tension.

"I'm not sure, son. Try the kitchen," replied Archer in a controlled voice. He had taken it upon himself to remain calm in the hopes that his family would do the same. The phone was always disappearing. Somehow it was never put back in its proper place, and nowadays, Archer simply was not in a position to go looking for it.

Archer's son walked briskly into the kitchen and found the phone. He dialed a number, then went into the study room and closed the door behind him. From the living room, Archer could hear his son talking in a hushed voice into the receiver. Even though he couldn't hear what his son was saying, Archer knew what the call was about. Bryan had been making phone calls all day since their visit to the neurosurgeon's office. While Archer's wife had been consumed with despair, his son had become consumed with denial.

Archer had lived his life honestly with a devout sense of responsibility to his family and his work. He had become well respected in his community, in particular for his charity. He was a 65-year-old tall man, with graying hair and a warm smile, and although many would say he had lived a good life, Archer did not see his life as complete. Despite what the doctors said, he felt within him a willingness to fight and a vitality of life that was not over. He had yet to attend his son's graduation from medical school and to hold his first grandchild in his arms. And so, Archer retreated deep into his faith and prayed.

After endless hours of research, Bryan found what he was looking for. As a medical student, he initially became concerned many months ago with his father's sudden difficulty walking. His father had begun to trip often, and he seemed to lose his balance frequently. Since childhood, Bryan had known his father to be a strong man, but Archer's hands had started to lose strength and his handwriting had deteriorated significantly. Bryan knew his father to love going out for walks with his mother, but now he had difficulty even making it to the bathroom. His father's body was stiff and he was experiencing numbness in his extremities.

Bryan knew these were bad signs. He urged his father to see a doctor many times, finally consulting with the family physician who then referred him on to a neurologist.

"We need to get an MRI to see what is going on," the neurologist said. An MRI was performed, and the neurologist uttered a word most feared in the modern era— "cancer". Archer's neurologist sat down and explained the condition.

"Your MRI shows that you have a very dangerous malignant spinal cord tumor involving the upper cervical spine and extending into the lower brainstem. The tumor is inside your spinal cord," said the neurologist. "You will need to see a neurosurgeon…as soon as possible. I will refer you to a neurosurgeon close by."

Tension built as Archer's appointment with the local neurosurgeon, Dr. Jackson, drew close. Upon seeing Archer's films, Dr. Jackson immediately recognized the gravity of the situation.

"Your neurologist was correct. You have a malignant spinal cord tumor extending into your lower brainstem," said the neurosurgeon gravely.

"So what are you going to do to fix it?" Archer asked.

"Well, I'm sorry to say that your condition is terminal. There really isn't anything I can do to help you Archer," said the neurosurgeon.

"What do you mean there's nothing you can do…can't you operate?" Archer was astonished. "There must be something you can do to help," he pleaded.

"I really am sorry, Archer. I know this is a lot of information to absorb, but you need to understand that there really is nothing I can do…" Dr. Jackson turned away from Archer, poised to exit the exam room. He momentarily paused, and said hesitantly, "Perhaps you should consult with another neurosurgeon with more specialized skills—for a second opinion, I mean. But I stand by what I said, your condition is terminal and there is nothing I can do to help."

The whole family was devastated with the news. Bryan researched his father's condition and knew that the neurosurgeon was right—his father's condition was very serious and not much could be done. He could not accept his father's death, however, and began researching neurosurgeons in Houston with the hopes that one may be able to help his father. He talked to many people in the community and made endless phone calls in an attempt to find neurosurgeons who would be willing to manage Archer's disease. It is not easy to find the right doctor when you need one. He had called all his family members and friends that lived in Houston, all to no avail. Bryan nearly gave up his search. He sat at his desk in the study room and rubbed his temples.

Suddenly, the phone rang. Bryan picked up the receiver. A loud, shrill voice spoke, and Bryan immediately recognized it as belonging to his great Aunt Donna. She was a nice old lady, with big thick glasses, a sunny disposition, and the hint of a Southern twang in her accent.

"Bryan! This is your Aunt Donna callin'. Your cousin Sammy told me you were lookin' for a brain surgeon in town?"

"Yes, Aunt Donna, a neurosurgeon. Do you know about anyone who you can recommend?" replied Bryan.

"Well, there is a doctor that I've heard of...you remember your second cousin Mason? Well his wife had some sort of condition…I don't quite remember what it was—you know how it is at this age…things are always slippin' my mind. Anyways, it was something to do with her head and her back and I just remember she couldn't use her legs all of a sudden…such a sad story really dear. The doctors said there was nothing they could do for her! They saw so many doctors too. Oh, it was so sad dear," said Aunt Donna.

Bryan rolled his eyes in frustration. He didn't have time for sadness—he had enough of his own. "Aunt Donna…I have a lot of work to do…perhaps we can talk another time?" said Bryan.

"Well now wait just a second. Mason's wife heard about a brain surgeon in Houston—I believe his name was AJ? No—maybe Dr. Ajay Bindal? Anyways she had her surgery done by him and she's doing well now. You really should see about this brain surgeon," said Aunt Donna. She continued the conversation, rambling about this and that, as always. But Bryan barely heard what she said. His mind was still focused on what Aunt Donna had said about the neurosurgeon she had heard of.

As soon as his Aunt was finished talking, Bryan scrambled to research Dr. Bindal on his computer. As Bryan continued to research, his mother walked in with a plate full of muffins and cookies. She always kept herself busy with cooking and baking when she was upset. She looked over her son's shoulder and saw his computer screen.

"Who is this Dr. Bindal you're looking up?"

she asked.

"He's a neurosurgeon Aunt Donna told me about," replied Bryan. "I think we should see him to ask for a second opinion on Dad's condition. He may give us a different answer than the first neurosurgeon did." His mother's face immediately brightened.

"Do you think this neurosurgeon can help your father?" asked Bryan's mother eagerly.

"I don't know," said Bryan, "but I hope so." Whatever this doctor could do for his father, he was willing to take. Bryan propositioned the idea of making an appointment to see Dr. Bindal to his father.

"There's another neurosurgeon in town that Aunt Donna recommended over the telephone. He may have a more specialized skill set. I think we should have him evaluate you," said Bryan.

Archer was silent at first. He worried that Dr. Bindal would give the same news the first neurosurgeon did, and his family would suffer devastation yet again. But Archer knew that he had many years to live—he felt it in his soul. Perhaps this other neurosurgeon would be able to help him. He began a short prayer, envisioning God and heaven. He envisioned his future, his family, and good fortune. He was interrupted by his son's voice.

"This may be our only chance, Dad. You heard what the first doctor said," implored Bryan.

After a few moments of contemplation, he

said, "Alright son, let's make an appointment."

Bryan called Dr. Ajay Bindal's office and made an appointment for his father. After making the call, he sat back in his chair. He hoped that it would be the last phone call he'd have to make for a while. Now, all he could do was wait.

As the elevator reached the second floor of the doctor's office building, Archer remained unusually calm. He could sense the anxiety crippling his wife and son, yet somehow, he felt at peace. With his vision in mind, Archer had a good feeling about the future, and he was positive he would receive good news from the doctor.

The elevator doors opened, and Archer slowly stepped off the elevator with the help of his wife and son. He walked slowly and with great difficulty towards Dr. Bindal's office, located around the corner of the elevator lobby. Even with the aid of a walker and support from his wife on his right and his son on his left, by this point, Archer could barely make it to Dr. Bindal's office. His movements were spastic and he was severely crippled.

Archer and his family entered Dr. Bindal's office. The office was bright, and he was filled with a sense of strength and hope. His son signed him in with the receptionist at the front desk as Archer took a seat in the waiting room. The receptionist handed Archer forms to fill out. He attempted to reach for a pen, but his hands were stiff and immovable.

"I'll do it, Dad," said Bryan, as he helped him fill out the necessary paperwork, including Archer's patient history and demographic forms. Bryan handed the forms and a copy of Archer's MRI to the receptionist, and then they waited patiently.

CHAPTER TWO

It was 6:50 AM when Dr. Ajay Bindal turned his car into the hospital parking garage. He parked in his usual spot, which, despite not being reserved, always seemed to be left open for him. He stepped out of his car and retrieved his briefcase and white lab coat, which had been placed neatly and carefully in the trunk so as to inhibit the creation of any creases or wrinkles. He was a big, quiet man, with a comforting face—the kind that made you feel safe.

Dr. Bindal had a meeting to attend at 7:00 AM. He was involved in several hospital leadership committees with the hopes of improving the hospital's quality and efficiency. He had always felt that everyone should strive to make a difference in whichever way they can. It was just last night that he was explaining to his daughter, Mohini, who had recently attained a leadership position in a high school organization, that leadership was an important quality to possess.

"We are all one piece of a big pie, and we all have our role," said Dr. Bindal. "It is the summation of our individual leadership efforts that makes America great."

As Chairman of the Credentials and Medical Ethics Committee, Dr. Bindal was responsible for physician privileges and monitoring physician competence and ethics. After the meeting was over, he proceeded to his office to begin his clinic.

Dr. Bindal walked across the street to the hospital office building, then took the elevator to the second floor. He stepped off the elevator and briskly turned the corner of the elevator lobby and entered his office through the side door.

"Good morning, Dr. Bindal!" said his office manager cheerfully. Her voice had the hint of an East Texas accent in it. He looked over to see Lana sitting at her desk. With a loyal commitment to patient care, Lana was a true embodiment of "southern hospitality".

"Good morning, Lana," he replied. He walked into his private office, where his computer had been turned on by his office staff. A patient's chart was already sitting on his desk.

"Remember Dr. Bindal, today is the day the local news channel is sending their news anchor over to film the post-operative results of Ms. Yates."

Dr. Bindal's recalled his patient, Julia Yates, whom he had recently performed surgery on. The hospital had become interested in her surgery due to the fascinating pathologic nature of the case.

Clinic began, and Julia walked in. Upon seeing Dr. Bindal, she broke into a big smile and greeted him warmly. Julia was ecstatic—for the first time in years, she was able to smile and converse with people. She worked in customer service and loved to interact with others, but for more than six years, she had suffered from a relentless facial twitch, day and night, preventing her from eating, talking, and even seeing. The right side of her face had been twitching uncontrollably, so much so that in the morning she would wake up and her face would "feel sideways". The spasms had made it difficult for her to work with people, and she had tried different medications, even Botox, but none prevailed.

Julia finally scheduled a visit to Dr. Bindal's office. He immediately recognized her as suffering from hemifacial spasms due to compression of a nerve in the brain from an artery. The condition affects only one in a million people, and Dr. Bindal is one of the few neurosurgeons who performs the surgery to correct the problem for good.

Dr. Bindal performed surgery on Julia. He created a small hole in the back of her skull and placed a sponge between an artery and nerve, protecting the nerve so that the symptoms would go away. Three days after the surgery, the spasms stopped.

Julia was now at Dr. Bindal's office for a routine post-operative check-up. Almost immediately after her arrival, an extremely well dressed, attractive woman walked into Dr. Bindal's office, followed by two women with large cameras. The woman approached Dr. Bindal and flashed a charismatic smile.

"Hi Dr. Bindal, I'm Rita McGovern. We're going to shoot Julia's post-operative results today." Rita McGovern possessed all the glitz and glamour one would expect of a premier news reporter. Her camera crew followed her closely as she navigated her way to Julia's exam room.

"I'm going to stand on this side of the room with the camera crew, while you talk to Julia just as you would normally," she said to Dr. Bindal.

"Should I look at the camera?" asked Dr. Bindal.

"Pretend like we aren't even here," said Rita McGovern. She flashed her captivating smile again. She took permission from Julia, and then began to film the appointment.

Dr. Bindal performed the routine reflex and strength tests on Julia. He was glad to see that her twitching had completely ceased.

"Thank you, Dr. Bindal," said Julia repeatedly. "You've really made a difference in my life. Every morning I wake up, I touch my face, begin talking, and am thrilled to find that the twitching has ceased. At night, I no longer feel the fluttering in my face, and it has made a big difference."

Dr. Bindal loved successful outcomes, as any

doctor does. But sometimes, successful outcomes are difficult, if not impossible, to come by.

The wait was short, but it felt like an eternity. After a few minutes, Archer's name was called by the receptionist. They were led into the office past the waiting room and were seated in the first exam room on the left. Archer took a seat on the cool, blue exam table. His wife and son sat down on the two chairs that were placed across from the doctor's chair. Surrounding them on the walls were posters describing different neurological conditions. Archer sighed. He knew that his son was consumed with worry. Had this been a normal day, Bryan would have been devouring the information presented on the posters, yet today Bryan sat stiff in his chair biting his nails.

"*I wish he wasn't so worried*," thought Archer to himself. "*If only my son had a little more faith*."

Archer's mother looked at a poster on the wall beside her. "What does all this mean, Bryan?" she asked, pointing to some words.

Bryan stood to look at the poster. "It's describing basic nervous system anatomy," he explained. "The brain and spinal cord are protected by multiple layers. There's the 'pia', which 'piously' follows the surface of the brain and spinal cord. It is so thin that you can't see it with the naked eye. Then there's the 'arachnoid' on top of that. The 'arachnoid' layer is 'spider-like'. On top of that is the thick 'dura', so called because of its durability. Cerebrospinal fluid, which provides shock absorption and buffering space, flows within the arachnoid layer. The brain and spinal cord with all these layers exist within the skull and spinal bones." Bryan paused for a moment, and before he could continue, they heard a knock on the door.

A medical assistant in the office entered the room and checked Archer's vital signs. A few moments later, the doctor walked in.

Dr. Bindal walked into the first exam room and found a young man and an elderly woman seated to the side, both appearing quite anxious. Anxiety was common amongst the patients in his office, and he knew that it was his job to comfort them in any way that he could. Surprisingly, however, the elderly gentleman seated on the exam table appeared quite calm. "Hello, I'm Dr. Ajay Bindal," he said to the patient and his family. "What can I do for you today?"

"It's nice to meet you Dr. Bindal. I'm Archer, and this is my wife and my son. My son is a medical student right now," Archer said, with pride. Archer's son introduced himself to Dr. Bindal, and proceeded to explain his father's situation to the doctor. Archer let his son do all the talking- medical terminology confused him, and his son knew more about his condition than he did himself.

Dr. Bindal reviewed Archer's films, asked him questions about his medical history and the history of his condition, and performed an exam. He tested

Archer's strength in his arms and legs, and then tested Archer's reflexes. Archer was severely handicapped—he completely lacked strength in his legs, so much so that Dr. Bindal felt it was an "act of God" that Archer was even able to make the short distance from the elevator to the office without a wheelchair. Archer's films showed that he had classic radiographic findings for a malignant tumor of the spinal cord that extended into his brainstem. These findings were confirmed by the radiologist who was very confident of the likely diagnosis.

"This tumor is damaging your spinal cord nervous tissue and is paralyzing you," explained Dr. Bindal to Archer and his family. "Left alone, this tumor will take your life."

"So what can we do?" asked Archer.

"Well Archer, my advice is that excision of the tumor is unlikely. There is a high chance that the tumor is malignant. We need to biopsy the tumor so that we can plan radiation and chemotherapy. In order to biopsy it, we would have to open the spinal cord at its most dangerous point near the brainstem. It is very likely that you would suffer further neurologic loss of function and even death from the operation."

"What kind of neurologic loss of function?" asked Archer.

"You could lose control of your ability to breathe and require a ventilator," replied Dr. Bindal. "You could be 'locked-in', meaning you would be awake, but completely unable to move your arms, legs, or any other muscles in your body. You would not be able to communicate with anyone, and you would only be able to blink and move your eyes."

"I see," said Archer, his heart sinking in his chest. He had hoped the doctor would have better news for him. "What do you suggest I do, Dr. Bindal?"

Dr. Bindal sighed. "Well, you have the option of simply letting the tumor take its course, and enjoy what time you have."

"So, how much time do you think I have?" asked Archer.

"Oh, probably three months to a year," Dr. Bindal responded.

Archer was shocked. The doctor's blatantly honest words cut deep into his soul. This wasn't what he had expected the doctor to say. "No... that's not true," spoke Archer. "You see, my palm reader says that I have a long lifeline." He raised his hand and displayed it to the doctor, pointing to a crease in his palm. "I believe in God and I have faith that I'm going to live many more years."

"Well, science says otherwise." Dr. Bindal responded. He always felt it was important to be blunt and direct with patients so that they don't get false expectations. "Surgery is an option, but it comes with serious risk."

Archer and his family sat silent for a few

moments. Then, with his vision of God in his mind and faith in his heart, he spoke. "I would like to proceed with the surgery."

Archer and his family went home. They sat at the kitchen table and ate lunch prepared by Archer's wife. The sound of forks and spoons against their plates resonated through the silent air. Bryan could barely bring himself to eat. His father's appointment with the doctor was playing over and over in his mind. *"Three months to a year,"* the doctor had said. *"Further neurologic loss of function and even death from the operation."*

If his father's death was a likely outcome from the operation, perhaps three months to a year was the best they had. Was proceeding with the surgery the correct decision? *"Maybe we should take some time to think about it…"* thought Bryan. A thousand thoughts continued to whirl through Bryan's mind as he sat at the table.

Finally, his father spoke. "What are you thinking, son?" asked Archer.

Bryan didn't know how to respond. He wasn't sure he quite understood his thoughts himself. His mind was full of conflict and doubts.

"I was just thinking…I mean maybe we made a decision too quickly," Bryan said carefully. "Maybe we should just take a day to think about it, or to talk about it."

"Talk about what?" asked Archer.

"You know, about whether or not surgery is the right move..." said Bryan.

"What are you suggesting?" Bryan's mother asked. Bryan didn't know what he was suggesting. He sighed.

"I'm not sure. Maybe we should see another doctor...see what another doctor has to say," he responded. His father looked up at him, then put his fork down.

"I don't think that's necessary," Archer said confidently. "I think we should just stick to this doctor we just saw. I'm comfortable with him."

"Why? Maybe another doctor will have a different opinion or something. I just think we may be rushing into this operation..."

"I'm okay with the doctor we saw today, son. He seemed confident, and composed. I know this is difficult, son, but I have a good feeling about this surgery. Everything will be okay," responded Archer.

Bryan dropped the conversation. His father was stubborn—once he had made up his mind, it was difficult to convince him otherwise. His father seemed set on the surgical option. Bryan worried about the possibility of his father suffering further neurologic damage. He felt his father did not quite understand the gravity of the situation, and his decision to proceed with surgery was made hastily on the basis of what may be misplaced faith. Bryan just hoped that his father's feelings about the surgery were right, and that everything would be okay.

CHAPTER THREE

At 6:00 AM, Dr. Bindal turned his car into the hospital parking garage. He pulled out his briefcase and white lab coat from the trunk, perfectly folded as usual. He took the elevator to the second floor and entered his office, where he grabbed his patient charts and films for the day. He then made his way to the recovery wing of the hospital, where he greeted the nurses at the desk warmly.

"Good morning, Sylvia. How is everything today?"

"Very good Dr. Bindal, very good!" she said cheerfully.

He smiled in response. The nurses and staff greeted him warmly as he walked through the hallways.

Dr. Bindal made rounds on his previous day's patients. After he ensured that each of his patients was recovering successfully, he opened the door to the doctor's lounge and walked in.

The lounge was spacious, with comfortable sofas, television sets, and tables. To one side, two men in dark green scrubs were seated at one of the tables, their heads locked, engaged in a deep, intense discussion in a somewhat argumentative fashion. At the other end of the room, a middle-aged gentleman dressed in scrubs as well looked up from his patient's charts.

"Hey, Ajay, how's it going?" Dr. Bindal recognized him as the neurologist who would be working with him today.

"Good morning, Bob." He gestured to the two men at the table. "What's going on over there?"

"Oh, just a friendly argument over the best course of treatment for a patient...you know how it is..."

Dr. Bindal laughed as he turned towards the locker room, where he changed his clothes into a pair of scrubs identical to those of the other doctors in the lounge.

A young nurse with large glasses and hair tied neatly back in a tight bun peered over her clipboard at Archer. She continued to fire questions at him in an assertive tone.

"Did you have anything to eat or drink after

midnight?"

"He didn't," his wife interjected. Archer shot a glance at his wife.

"I can speak for myself, you know. They haven't put me under yet." Archer knew his wife and son were nervous, but he couldn't help but find them a little overbearing. Archer and his family had arrived at the hospital's pre-operative wing at 6:30 in the morning. He asked the priest from his church to accompany them to the hospital that morning for moral support. Archer was scheduled to be the doctor's first surgery for the day. They signed in, and a nurse brought them to a pre-op room, or cubicle, which was separated from others by curtains. The pre-op holding area was a busy place. There were people bustling here and there, doctors giving nurses orders, nurses asking patients questions, and patients talking nervously with their families. Archer was told to change into a hospital gown and was given an identification wristband. Then, the endless questions began.

"Do you have allergies to any medications?" asked the nurse.

"Not that I know of."

"Okay. And are you on any medications now?"

Archer sighed. He didn't mind all these questions, but he felt his wife and son were becoming increasingly anxious. After Archer finally answered the last of the nurse's questions, a bald-headed man in scrubs walked in.

"Are you gonna be one of my doctors?" asked Archer.

"Yes sir, I'm the anesthesiologist," responded the doctor in a radiant voice. "I have a few questions to ask you before we continue to prep you for surgery. When was the last time you had something to eat or drink?"

"He already answered that question..." remarked Archer's wife in a disgruntled voice.

"Well, we like to double check ma'am. I'm sorry but I have to ask all these questions." The anesthesiologist turned his attention back to Archer. "Now, when was the last time you had something to eat or drink?"

"Last night at around six o'clock in the evening," responded Archer.

After Archer finished answering all of the anesthesiologist's questions, the nurses placed an IV and put stockings and thigh-high sequential compression boots, to prevent deep vein thrombosis, on Archer.

Dr. Bindal made his way through the bright halls of the hospital towards the pre-op area. He entered the pre-op wing and walked over to Archer's room. Archer was lying on a pre-op bed surrounded by his wife, son, and a priest.

"Hi Archer, how are you?" asked Dr. Bindal in a calm and composed voice. He knew that patients and their families at this time were at the height of their anxiety. Patients knew they were about to be cut open, and they often had scary feelings about the scalpel, anesthesia, and the uncertainty of whether or not they will wake-up after surgery.

"Are you ready for your surgery?" he asked Archer.

"Absolutely," replied Archer in a confident manner. Archer's lack of worry surprised Dr. Bindal yet again.

"Do you have any questions before we continue?"

"No, but I wanted to ask you—do you believe in God, Dr. Bindal?" Dr. Bindal recalled Archer's firm belief in his faith from their conversation in his office.

"Archer, I'm a firm believer in the power of faith based healing," replied Dr. Bindal with a smile.

"Oh good. Would you be willing to pray with me before the operation?" Archer indicated to the priest standing at his side.

"Of course."

The priest took Archer's hands in his left hand and Dr. Bindal's hand in his other. Archer lay in the gurney and looked up. He saw the priest, his family, and the doctor hovering over him, like angels looking down from heaven. The priest began a small prayer.

"Dear Lord, our Father in Heaven, we pray that you work your miracle of healing and guide this physician's hands," began the priest. He continued the prayer, and then finished with "Amen."

Dr. Bindal turned his attention to Archer's family.

"When I'm done with the operation, I will catch you in the waiting room," he said. Dr. Bindal then left for the operating room.

In the operating room, a husky, middle-aged, female scrub nurse with short blonde hair and a commanding personality was setting up the instrument tables. She opened the instrument packets and began arranging them to her discretion, along with preparing medications, drapes, gloves, and other necessary equipment. The process takes nearly an hour—she had begun at seven o'clock in the morning.

The operating room was large and spacious with white walls and bright white lights. There was an aura of intensity brought on by the presence of large monitors and technological equipment. The room was cold, with the temperature set at 64 degrees Fahrenheit, yet everyone in the room wore a single layer of short-sleeved scrubs. Their dress would normally render people to shivers, but the intensity of the work performed in the operating room more often brings sweat.

The operating room and equipment were the epitome of human accomplishment. Everything that mankind has produced—from chemistry, biology, physics, and mathematics, to computers, software, manufacturing, and metalworking—all culminated at this one point for the benefit of one person—the patient. In this moment, a person's life was at stake, and only the best of the best would be used to save him. The hands of millions of people around the world play a part in a patient's outcome, and the patient's life is defined by the best that we as a species can produce.

More nurses and other hospital staff began to bustle in and out of the room as the preparation ensued. As the time to begin the surgery neared, the surgeon walked in. The scrub nurse looked up and said in a voice muffled by her surgical mask, "Good morning Dr. Bindal. Have you seen the patient in pre-op yet?"

"Good morning Jenna. I just got back from the pre-op holding area. They should be bringing the patient in shortly," he replied.

He stood near the large monitors to the side and began to pull up the patient's MRI films on the computer which had a 65-inch-high resolution screen allowing for optimal viewing. He then sat in one of the chairs near the entrance to the operating room and began to prepare.

Surgery is a skill that requires the utmost

precision and planning. While the nurses prepared the instruments and equipment, Dr. Bindal began to prepare his mind for the surgery. He mentally visualized how he would do the surgery—how the patient will be positioned, how the incision will be done, how the operation will be performed. He recounted and refreshed his mind, and he checked the patient's chart for details. Planning was, after all, the most important part of the procedure.

"Every battle is won before it's ever fought." -Sun Tzu

A while after Dr. Bindal had left the pre-op holding area, Archer was finally ready to be transported to the operating room.

"We're ready to take you to the operating room now, Archer," said Betsy, the circulating nurse. She turned to Archer's family. "You can wait in the waiting area until his operation is over. Now is the time for hugs and kisses."

Archer looked at his wife and son. The worry on their faces was overwhelming.

"Everything will be alright. I'll see you after the operation. Don't worry," he said gently. A tear ran down his wife's face. Archer couldn't bear the sight of his wife crying.

"Don't worry," he repeated. "Have some faith. The surgery will be successful—I know it will be."

"We are praying for you," she said. "It will be fine." Bryan nodded in accordance.

"We'll see you soon, dad. Good luck."

Archer smiled. His wife bent down and gave him a kiss on the cheek. He turned back to the nurse waiting to take him to the OR.

"You can take me to the operating room now," he said.

Betsy took hold of Archer's gurney and began moving it slowly towards the operating room. Bryan watched as his father was led away. He turned to his mother and gave her a reassuring smile.

"Let's go to the waiting room now," he said to his mom.

Arm in arm, Bryan led his mother to the waiting room, where they joined countless anxiety stricken family members of other patients. And so, the nervous wait began.

After a few moments, Archer was brought into the operating room. Betsy wheeled him in on a gurney straight from the pre-op holding area.

"Wow, this room is so bright, I feel like I'm entering heaven!" Archer remarked.

The anesthesiologist chuckled. "Looks like the sedatives are kicking in."

Betsy positioned his gurney parallel to the operating table. Due to Archer's lack of strength, a few strong male attendants assisted him in moving onto the operating table.

"Okay Archer, you can start counting to ten now," said the anesthesiologist, as he placed a large mask over Archer's mouth and nose. Archer began counting as he inhaled the anesthetic through the mask.

As Archer was put to sleep, the anesthesiologist began to place various leads and monitors on him. The anesthesiologist placed a tube down Archer's throat that would allow him to breathe during the surgery (i.e. intubation). After he was intubated, the anesthesia assistant, Tim, helped place more monitors to watch his CO_2 output, his temperature, and other things.

"Go ahead and put the BIS monitor on now and secure his eyes," said the anesthesiologist to Tim.

"What does the BIS monitor do again?" asked Tim. He was new to his job, so he was still getting used to all the monitoring equipment used in neurosurgical procedures.

"It allows us to keep track of the patient's level of consciousness," explained the anesthesiologist. Together, they secured Archer's eyes with tape and goggles to prevent injury.

A monitoring team, consisting of a neurologist and a monitoring technician arrived to place more leads and to overlook changes in the patient's monitoring potentials, including EMG, SSEP, MEP, and BAER, all which indicate nerve injury or damage.

"What do all of those leads do?" asked Tim.

"These leads connect to these monitors over here," explained the anesthesiologist, pointing to monitors to the side. "They allow us to monitor the patient's neurologic status. This squiggly line is the waveform. As long as it's not flat, that's good. If we lose the signals and the waveform goes flat, then we worry about having caused nerve injury or damage. That's bad!"

Due to the location of Archer's tumor, major shifts in his blood pressure could occur during the operation. The anesthesiologist inserted an arterial line into an artery in Archer's wrist to monitor his blood pressure changes. A central line was also placed into a vein leading into the heart to allow the initiation of high doses of fluid resuscitation in case it was needed.

"How do you want the operating table positioned, Dr. Bindal?" asked Jenna, the scrub nurse.

"Lateral oblique, thirty degrees, head right here" he responded, pointing to the exact seemingly auspicious spot on the floor which had been strategically selected as the location where the lighting, equipment and microscope all reached perfectly.

Anesthesia technicians were called to readjust the table to the lateral oblique position. The men were big and burly, with body structures similar to those of football linebackers. They changed the patient's position to lateral oblique—a precise angle of rotation, and then the patient was secured with gel pads, pillows, and tape to keep him secure.

Dr. Bindal looked at the table, and thought for a moment.

"Back up, 15 degrees," he said in an assertive voice. The table was lifted slightly. Dr. Bindal scanned the table again. Everything had to be perfect. After a few seconds of scrutiny, he decided the table's position was correct. He began to prepare the back of Archer's neck for the surgery by marking out where he would begin the incision. The scrub nurse prepared the skin where the mark was made with Betadine and alcohol. Dr. Bindal ensured that the position of his patient's head was proper to allow access for the equipment he would be using and that the lights were positioned properly on top of the table. Then, he put on his headlight and left the operating room to wash his hands.

Immediately outside the operating room, in large, long sinks, Dr. Bindal washed his hands thoroughly. In his mind he pondered and rehearsed the operation. He questioned if there was something that he was missing. This was the last chance to make any alterations in the surgical plan. Then, he re-entered the operating room.

"Towel," he commanded, and Jenna handed him a towel to dry his hands. She gave him his gown and helped him into gloves. Now, Dr. Bindal was sterile and ready to begin operating. He re-marked the incision site on his patient's neck and used bright blue towels to square off the incision site, giving enough gaps for any adjustments that may be needed. He then placed a plastic iodinated barrier, or IOBAN, and then a drape on top of that. The drape covered Archer's face and the rest of his body, creating a sterile field.

"Good thing the drapes are opaque so we don't have to look at his face," said Tim, as the surgical drapes hid Archer's humanity from the surgeon's vision.

Meanwhile, Jenna brought her table of instruments and began to set up all the devices that would be used frequently. She placed the suction tube in front of her, and the nitrogen gas powered drill, which rotates at up to 100,000 rpm to her right. To her left, she placed the two electrocautery devices, the bovie and bipolar, which are used to stop bleeding. The nurse rearranged the other instruments to surround her such that she could reach around herself and know the exact location of any of the numerous instruments that she had laid in front of her.

"Local," said Dr. Bindal.

The scrub nurse handed him 10 cc of local anesthesia in a small needle, used also to help reduce bleeding at the incision site. Now, finally, the patient was ready.

"Dr. Bindal, the patient's blood pressure is down. Now would be a good time for incision," said the anesthesiologist. Dr. Bindal nodded and took a deep breath.

"Ten blade."

Jenna handed Dr. Bindal a scalpel, and he made his first incision into the back of Archer's neck. Archer's blood pressure and pulse took a sudden surge. Bright red blood gushed from the incision, dripping down the sides of the drapes.

Betsy looked at the monitors, confused for a moment. "I thought the patient was under anesthesia, but it looks like he's feeling your knife," she said.

"He may be asleep, but he's still alive," responded Dr. Bindal. Archer's blood pressure and pulse normalized as Dr. Bindal began the operation.

Archer's wife took a sudden gasp of air. "I think they just began the operation," she said to her son. "What do you think?"

"They are probably preparing Dad for the operation, and they may have begun cutting already," replied Bryan. He was glad he was a medical student—it made reading about the operation a lot easier. It helped that he could understand all the medical terminology, and he felt more calm knowing exactly what was going to happen to his father. Bryan's mother, on the other hand, was not so calm.

"You're sure he won't feel anything, right?" she asked.

"No, mom, he won't feel a thing. They put him to sleep," he responded. "*I just hope Dad wakes up*," he thought to himself. Bryan sighed. He hoped everything was going well so far. The doctor had been clear about the risks this surgery posed. "*Calm down, Bryan. Now's not the time for second thoughts…*" It was nine o'clock now, and Bryan was mentally exhausted. He began to bite his nails again—a bad habit of his during times of worry. He turned his attention to his mother, who was sitting silently in the seat next to him. Her hair was a mess, and she had large bags under her eyes.

"Mom, maybe you should take a short nap. We have a few hours of just waiting…" he said tentatively.

"I can't sleep. I'm not tired," she responded immediately.

Bryan dropped the subject. He understood. He couldn't sleep either.

"Self-retainer," commanded Dr. Bindal. Jenna handed him a self-retaining retractor with ratcheted ends, used to pry open the incision site. Using the bovie cautery device, he began to dissect his way down to the spinous processes of the cervical spine, reaching all the way down to the bottom/back end of the skull. Dr. Bindal could now clearly visualize the C1 and C2 cervical vertebrae due to their unique anatomy. He stripped the muscles laterally using the bovie device, exposing the cervical spine. Then, a rongeur instrument was used to clip off the spinous processes.

"Microscope in, headlight off, table down to waist height," said Dr. Bindal.

The large overhanging microscope was brought in at the perfect angle. His head light was turned off, and the table was brought down. Dr. Bindal set the microscope to the proper optical depth and distance, focusing in on Archer's spine.

"Drill."

Jenna handed him a Midas Rex acorn drill bit. This was a critical moment. With the high spinning drill, one slip of the hand could paralyze and/or permanently maim Archer. Handling of the drill requires tremendous experience, confidence, and coordination. With the drill in his right hand and suction in the other, Dr. Bindal began drilling the lamina of the cervical spine and lower skull under microscopic guidance.

Using a Cloward punch, like a nails cutter, the remaining bone of the lamina was removed to expand the opening. Again, Dr. Bindal had the punch in his right hand and suction in the other, sometimes alternating hands. A good neurosurgeon is partially ambidextrous. With precision and coordination, he clipped fractions of a millimeter of the lamina bone at a time.

Dr. Bindal placed fibrillar and bone wax along the edges of the lamina to prevent bleeding. It was important to keep bleeding from occurring in the spinal cord region where hemostasis is essential.

"15 blade."

He incised the dura, or the lining of the brain and spinal cord. The dura was tacked up and out of the way, exposing the underlying arachnoid layer filled with cerebrospinal fluid. Immediately, spinal fluid began to pour out, and beneath, the spinal cord and brainstem were visible. Dr. Bindal asked for his motorized chair.

"Your throne, Dr. Bindal," joked Betsy as she brought in the chair. The chair was a highly specialized motorized chair that moves up and down and provides adjustable armrests, allowing for long operations to be performed. It was Dr. Bindal's special chair—only he used it.

Dr. Bindal secured his chair in its proper position. "Lights out," he said. The lights in the operating room were turned off, so that only the light of the microscope shined brightly and directly on the incision site.

The chattering in the operating room ceased. The surgical team knew that this was the time to focus—it was the peak time of the surgery, where the most vulnerable parts of the body were exposed and the danger of injury to patient was at its highest. By this time, the large screen TV had been set up to project what Dr. Bindal could see through the microscope. Everyone turned to the screen to watch what was happening in the millimeters wide opening in the back of Archer's neck.

Bryan could hardly tolerate it any longer—the endless waiting with nothing to do. He reached into his bag and took out one of his medical books—a thick, hard-covered textbook on pathology. He flipped it open to the bookmarked page and began reading. He read through a few pages, then realized that he had absorbed absolutely nothing. *"That's the worst…"* he thought to himself, *"not having anything to do, yet not wanting to do anything either."*

He turned to his mother, who was sitting in the exact same position as she was hours earlier. She hadn't moved even one inch. He wondered what she was thinking.

"Do you want me to get you something, mom?" he asked her, gently.

She turned her head towards him slowly. "No," she responded. Bryan sighed. He put his arm around his mother, and she smiled weakly at him.

The door to the waiting area swung open. Bryan looked up quickly, hoping that maybe, just maybe, the surgery was already over—it was quicker than expected, and Dr. Bindal was here to tell him that his father would be okay.

A doctor in scrubs entered, and walked to the other side of the room to another family. Bryan turned back to his pathology textbook. *"Oh well,"* he thought to himself, and he continued to read the words on the page, not once stopping to understand a single sentence.

Dr. Bindal looked down at Archer's spinal cord and brainstem—glistening white with bright red arteries and purple veins coursing along the surface. It was pulsating—the spinal cord, the brainstem, the spinal fluid, the vessels—all pulsating with each beat of Archer's heart and every breath he took. Everyone in the room grew quiet, leaving only the sounds of the patient and machines resonating through the room. The monitors beeped with the beating of Archer's heart.

Tha dump...tha dump...tha dump

Archer's respiration echoed distantly. All of the machines supporting Archer's life sung in harmony.

Beep beep...beep beep...beep beep

Dr. Bindal listened carefully to the symphony of sounds, all creating the music of life. The clock on the wall ticked, linking him to the outside universe.

Tick tock...tick tock...tick tock

Dr. Bindal connected subconsciously to the rhythm, his own heartbeat and breaths in synchrony with Archer's. Like a monk in a deep trance, Dr. Bindal steadfastly remained focused on the surgery.

Even as a neurosurgeon, Dr. Bindal is filled with wonder at the sight of a living human brainstem. He peered down on Archer's brainstem through the small opening.

"Take a look at this," he gestured to the nurses. "Isn't it wonderful? Even if you've traveled to all of the most amazing places on Earth, you still haven't seen anything until you've seen a person's pulsating brainstem—it is the seat of the soul."

Tim stood and peered into the cavity from behind the drapes. "Why is the brainstem so important, that damage to it results in coma or death?" he asked.

"Well," started Dr. Bindal, "I think there's a reticulating network of super-controlling neural cells, if you will, that connect with other neurons through the brainstem, that in turn connect with every neuron above and below the brainstem. This network of controlling cells is likely the essence of who we are. Unless you knock off all these cells, consciousness is still intact, and the patient lives."

Betsy cut in. "Yes, but this patient's faith is very strong. I think he would say so long as he has his faith, he still lives." Dr. Bindal paused a moment to reflect on nurse Betsy's words. The room grew quiet again as he drew his attention back to the surgery.

Dr. Bindal's eyes scanned the opening through the microscope. This was the difficult part— the decision of where to make the opening in the spinal cord. A millimeter in the wrong spot, one wrong move, and Archer may never wake up again. There was but one pathway to the tumor, and Dr. Bindal had to find it. He looked back at the MRI scan, visualizing three-dimensionally in his mind the tumor sitting in front of him under the microscope.

"*Where do I open?*" he thought to himself. He had to plan an incision that would require the least amount of cauterization and avoid injury to the blood vessels. After a few moments of quick thinking, Dr. Bindal began to dissect through the exact center of the spinal cord.

Using microdissection tools and the microscope at its highest magnification, he carefully dissected through the spinal cord, straight to the tumor. A few moments later, the tumor was finally visible. It was distinctly different from the healthy tissue of Archer's spinal cord—the tumor was a dirty red-brown color, compared to the glistening white of the spinal cord. Dr. Bindal immediately removed a small biopsy sample, which the nurse placed in a small bottle. Another nurse took the bottle and left the operating room quickly for the pathology lab.

In the meantime, Dr. Bindal continued to work on the tumor. The phone rang a few minutes later. Betsy picked up the phone and put it on speaker.

"This is Dr. Butler, calling in frozen section results for Dr. Bindal," said a deep male voice over the speaker.

Dr. Bindal looked up from the surgical field briefly. "This is Dr. Bindal. Go ahead Dr. Butler," he responded from behind his surgical mask. He stopped his dissection to listen to the phone.

"The biopsy sample is consistent with a benign schwannoma."

Dr. Bindal's brow furrowed. "Thank you, Dr. Butler," he said slowly. He looked down at the microscopic opening. *"Benign schwannoma?"* he thought to himself. Dr. Bindal was momentarily confused. Such an occurrence was extremely rare—there were only a few reported cases in the literature of such a tumor in this location, and pathologic diagnosis from biopsies done at the time of surgery is often incorrect.

Dr. Bindal had a decision to make—if Archer's tumor was malignant, then he had to stop the surgery. Removing a malignant tumor would not cure Archer of the disease, and he would risk becoming maimed by surgery for no benefit. However, the pathologist suggested that the tumor was benign. Even though the tumor may be benign, if any tumor was left behind it would still grow back and take Archer's life. The only chance of helping Archer would be complete removal of the tumor now.

"The pathologist could be wrong though…" he thought. *"First, do no harm,"* Dr. Bindal recited to himself. It was the definition of non-maleficence, a rule by which all doctors must abide. *"If the frozen section analysis is indeed correct, then I have to remove it…"* he thought.

Suddenly, Archer's words rang through Dr. Bindal's ears. *"I believe in God and I have faith that I have many more years,"* Archer had said. Dr. Bindal felt a sudden compelling force pushing him to resect the tumor. The surgical team all stared at him, as he made his final decision.

"You heard the pathologist, let's take this tumor out then!" he said.

A technician brought in a YAG laser, which is used to burn tumor tissue while allowing doctors to minimize trauma to surrounding structures. The tumor shrinks and can then be peeled off from within the cavity it created, resulting in minimal trauma to the spinal cord. As he began to use the YAG laser to burn the tumor, Dr. Bindal constantly checked with the neuro monitoring team to ensure Archer was okay.

Dr. Bindal burned more and more tumor, constantly burning, cutting, and then resecting it. Burn, cut, dissect, resect—he continued the process for a long time, working out millimeter by millimeter of the tumor. The nurses watched nervously, fearful of any slip of the hand that could injure Archer. Dr. Bindal followed along the length of the tumor, all the way to Archer's brainstem. "*The tumor must be receiving its blood supply from somewhere, but where?*" he thought to himself. As he continued to cut, he realized the blood supply was from the superior most portion of the tumor, right in the deepest part of Archer's brainstem.

Suddenly, blood entered the surgical field, and he found himself having to cauterize. He began to worry about damaging the brainstem. He had reached deep into Archer's brainstem. Archer could suffer damage and become 'locked-in'. "*What if it's already too late?*" he wondered. "*Archer could already be paralyzed or maimed…Dear Lord, what am I doing?*" He looked at the surgical opening and took a moment to think, then proceeded with further resection. It was as if his

51

hands had been compelled to remove more tumor in order to achieve Archer's expectation of long survival. He continued to chase the tumor down to its last few cells, when a voice in the operating room, full of concern, suddenly interrupted him.

"Dr. Bindal, we've lost the waveform," said the monitoring technician.

Dr. Bindal looked up. For a moment, it seemed as if his entire medical career flashed before his eyes. The monitoring waves had stopped registering. Could there be brainstem injury, or is it just a technical failure? He had no way of knowing whether or not Archer could be suffering nerve damage. He looked back at the incision, and he realized that whatever it was that was compelling him to resect had ceased. He now had the strong sense to stop. He still worried that, perhaps, some tumor cells may still be retained that may allow for the tumor to regrow. *"Should I continue...?"* he asked himself. He had to make a quick decision—the monitoring had failed, and the operating room was now a world of endless possibilities.

He made the final decision that it was time to stop. Dr. Bindal controlled the last bit of bleeding, then used thrombin-soaked gelfoam to make sure there was no bleeding from the tumor bed. The surgical team gave a general sigh of relief, though tension remained since the results of the surgery were still unknown. How much damage did Archer sustain?

Dr. Bindal sewed the dura together with a running nurolon stitch. Then, he asked the anesthesiologist to perform Valsalva procedures, which consisted of manually squeezing the ventilator to increase pressures in the lungs, thus increasing pressures in the brain and transmitting massive pressure waves down the spinal column. The Valsalva procedures test the integrity of the dural closure. Leakage was present in a couple of spots, and Dr. Bindal sewed over them. He squirted fibrin glue over the stitches to seal it further.

Dr. Bindal closed the muscle, fascia, fat, and subcutaneous layers, and then finally, he stitched together the last layer of skin. Archer's operation was now complete. He remained intubated on a ventilator and was taken to the ICU since his level of consciousness was unknown.

When it was safe to leave Archer, Dr. Bindal made his way to the waiting area, where Archer's wife and son were waiting for news.

CHAPTER FOUR

The doors to the waiting room opened again, and this time, Dr. Bindal walked in. Archer's wife and son immediately stood as the doctor walked towards them.

"Everything went well," began Dr. Bindal.

Bryan and his mother breathed a quick sigh of relief. "*Thank God*," they thought to themselves.

"I got all the tumor out that I could see, but there's a possibility that there may be more tumor left on the top portion, so we will have to follow this," said Dr. Bindal. It was important for him to be completely honest with the patient's family. "We don't know what Archer's neurologic status is yet—we will have to wait and see. He may be a little worse at first, but I'm hoping that he will recover. The initial pathology suggested that it was a benign kind of tumor, which is amazing—as I had not expected that—but we will have to wait for the final pathology report for confirmation," he finished.

"Did you hear that?" Archer's wife said excitedly to her son. "It could be benign!" She turned to Dr. Bindal. "God bless you doctor! Praise the Lord!"

Dr. Bindal smiled. He hoped the final pathology report would confirm the benign nature of the tumor.

"We will observe Archer in the ICU. The first twenty-four hours will be the most critical time. Let's pray that we don't have any complications like bleeding or swelling," he continued. After he finished talking to Archer's family, he turned to leave the waiting room and made his way to the recovery room to examine Archer.

Dr. Bindal arrived in the recovery room shortly. A nurse indicated Archer's location, and Dr. Bindal quickly walked over to Archer's bedside. Archer was not awake. He was not moving, and appeared to be very sleepy. Dr. Bindal waited patiently, constantly re-examining Archer for any possible changes.

"Wake up, Archer. Can you please wiggle your toes and show me two fingers?" asked Dr. Bindal periodically. There was still no response. Dr. Bindal was becoming increasingly worried.

"What do you want to do, Dr. Bindal?" asked a nearby nurse.

"Well, his eyes are still closed, and he isn't fully awake. Let's give him some more time," he responded.

The wait in the recovery room was torturous—it was the moment of judgment for most doctors, as they eagerly wait to see the consequences of their actions in the operating room. Dr. Bindal was nervous—the surgery was risky, and he was concerned about the possibility of a "locked-in" syndrome, a blood clot, swelling, or injury to the spinal cord. He anxiously waited and wondered what would happen.

As time progressed and Archer still did not wake up, Dr. Bindal began to consider ordering an MRI scan. He gave Archer a little more time, but when Archer still did not wake up, he turned to the anesthesiologist.

"If he has a blood clot, then I need to go back and re-open his spinal cord. We need to make that decision now. Before I take him for an MRI scan, I want to reverse the narcotics with Narcan."

"Are you sure you want to do that?" asked the anesthesiologist, worriedly. "It can cause his blood pressure and pulse to rise suddenly…"

"Of course, I'm sure. Give it to him—it's important," replied Dr. Bindal with confidence.

"Alright, I'll give him a dose of Narcan," said the anesthesiologist. Dr. Bindal nodded, and the anesthesiologist pushed a dose of Narcan into Archer's IV.

Almost immediately, Archer's eyes fluttered open. He began to wake up, and Dr. Bindal quickly rushed to examine him, since the effects of Narcan lasted only a few minutes.

"Can you wiggle your toes and show me two fingers Archer?"

Everyone in the recovery room held their breath, as they watched Archer's feet and hands. At first, there was no movement.

"Can you wiggle your toes and show me two fingers Archer?" repeated Dr. Bindal, his imploring voice full of concern. He continued to stare at Archer's feet and hands. Seconds felt like years, and there was still no movement. Then, suddenly, a glimmer of movement caught Dr. Bindal's eyes. Archer managed to barely move his toes and lift two of his fingers. Dr. Bindal breathed a sigh of relief.

"That's very good Archer," said Dr. Bindal, relieved to find that Archer had not suffered worsening neurologic deficit. He turned to the nurse. "Let's hold on that MRI scan."

There was still some paperwork to be done before Dr. Bindal's day was over, and he went to his office to finish it. As he sat in his chair, writing notes in Archer's chart, Dr. Bindal felt an immense rush of relief and hoped that Archer would make a quick recovery.

Archer was stable now, and visitors were

allowed to come and see him. His wife and son came quickly from the waiting room. They rushed to his bedside, sobbing silently, with tears of joy in their eyes. Archer was still asleep (the effects of Narcan wear off quickly).

"So, he is okay then?" asked Archer's wife to the nearby nurse.

"Yes, he is. He is still heavily sedated, but he woke up momentarily when Dr. Bindal was examining him," responded the nurse in a gentle voice.

"Thank the Lord," she whispered. She closed her eyes and prayed that this would be the end of Archer's misery.

When Archer's condition was deemed stable enough, he was moved from the ICU to a regular recovery room. He continued to have weakness, so he stayed in the hospital for many weeks. With the help of physical therapy and rehabilitation, he slowly gained his strength and made a remarkable recovery. Although he still had difficulty walking, his ambulation had significantly improved. A few weeks after the operation was performed, Archer's final pathology returned. The pathologist reported the lesion as an intra-medullary cervical spinal cord schwannoma. Dr. Bindal was surprised (and relieved) to see that the pathologist who deemed the intra-operative sample to be a benign schwannoma was correct after all. Indeed, there are only a few reported cases in the literature of this diagnosis, which is a slow-growing tumor. Despite slower growth, however, Dr. Bindal worried that the tumor would continue to grow and still cause progressive neurologic dysfunction and death overtime.

CHAPTER FIVE

3 Months Later

The elevator reached the second floor of the hospital's office building. As the doors opened, Archer stepped off the elevator, this time not needing the help of his wife and son. He walked towards Dr. Bindal's office, one foot in front of the other, each landing on the floor with a confidence he had not felt in a long time. Though he had not regained his strength 100%, his movements were smooth, lacking the spasticity that inflicted him three months prior. The medical assistant took him and his family to the back and seated him in an exam room. Archer climbed onto the blue exam table, smiling at his wife and son.

Dr. Bindal walked into the exam room. Archer appeared cheerful and fulfilled as ever, though his family was clearly anxious for the results of the most recent MRI that had been taken. Dr. Bindal loaded the MRI into the computer and scrolled through the images. He squinted his eyes and looked closer at the screen. To his amazement, the MRI scan showed no evidence of any residual tumor.

"Well Archer, based on the images, it looks like there is no evidence of any tumor left!" he said. Archer's family breathed sighs of relief, and Archer looked at Dr. Bindal with a knowing smile.

"So, Dr. Bindal, how long do you think I'm going to live now?" he asked.

Dr. Bindal could not help but break into an incredulous smile. "Well Archer, it seems you were right. You are going to live a long, long time."

"Dr. Bindal, please accept this as a reminder of the power of faith to remove all obstacles," said Archer, as he handed the doctor a small religious token he had brought in a bag. The gift that Archer gave him lies on the desk in his office to this date.

PART II

PRAYER, SALVATION, ATONEMENT

CHAPTER ONE

Bay City, Texas—John and Stephanie's Apartment

John had all the time in the world. He wasn't too worried. He had thought about it many times—proposing to Stephanie—but the fear of rejection kept him hesitant. What if she wasn't ready for the commitment yet? He didn't want to push her. They had time. After all, they had only been dating for six months, and they had just recently made the decision to move in together.

Today marked their six-month anniversary, and John had a wonderful evening planned for them. It was a beautiful spring day, perfect for a night of romance. John had made reservations for them to eat at Stephanie's favorite restaurant, and then, perhaps, they would end the night with some drinks at their apartment.

John woke up early. He showered and got dressed, then drove himself to the firehouse. He arrived at eight o'clock, just in time for roll call.

"Alright John, I'm gonna have you checking out the engines today to make sure they're fully operational," said the Captain.

"Yes sir," replied John. He enjoyed his job. The life of a fireman was full of unexpected events, something that he enjoyed greatly. Serving the community was his passion, and he was proud to have devoted his life to the fire service.

John, along with the other firemen, began to check each of the fire engines and other equipment to ensure they were functioning properly. The paramedics arrived later in the morning to double check the medical equipment and to ensure all medications were accounted for. After all the equipment was checked, John and the other firemen began physical training—an essential part of being a fireman.

Hours of physical training had made John a strong man. He was tall, with short dark hair, bright blue eyes, a charming smile, and an amiable personality. At 28 years old, he was young and had many more years left. Now, he was looking forward to settling down and starting a family, and Stephanie was just the woman for him. All he had to do was gather the courage to propose.

The large, antique-style clock on the wall

chimed six times. Stephanie sat up in bed and looked out the bedroom window as she yawned. It was a beautiful day outside, perfect for a morning run. Birds were chirping, playfully chasing each other through the clear sky and drinking the nectar from blooming flowers. Stephanie was energetic—she enjoyed the outdoors and often went hiking, biking, and engaged in other outdoor sports. With long blonde hair and hazel green eyes, Stephanie was a beautiful 27-year-old woman with a gentle smile and a warm heart.

The pendulum on the wall clock swayed back and forth, its beat rhythmic and predictable. Stephanie took a deep breath and allowed the beating of her heart to match the progression of the pendulum on the clock.

Tick tock...tick tock...tick tock

As she looked through her window, her vision suddenly fogged. She frowned, blinking a couple of times until her vision cleared again.

"*Strange*," she thought to herself. "*I've never had problems with my vision before...it's probably nothing.*" Stephanie was a healthy woman, and she had no reason to be concerned. Aside from the headaches she had been having more recently, her health was in excellent condition.

After her morning jog, Stephanie returned to the apartment for a quick shower. She had just finished putting on a pair of jeans and a pink blouse, when the phone rang.

"Hey Stephanie! It's Sarah!" said a quirky

female voice on the other line. Sarah was Stephanie's best friend—they had been friends through high school and college. "I was wondering if you wanted to go catch a movie tonight."

"Oh I'm sorry Sarah…I have plans tonight," responded Stephanie apologetically.

"Plans?! What plans," asked Sarah. She was always very inquisitive.

"I'm going out with John tonight actually."

"Oooohh…with John, huh? Is he *ever* going to propose?!"

Stephanie sighed, exacerbated. She was wondering the exact same thing. She was absolutely sure that John was the man for her, and she knew that John felt the same way, yet somehow, he seemed to be dragging his feet on the proposal.

"How could I possibly know," she responded flatly. "He hasn't mentioned anything in particular, if that's what you're asking."

"Oh, I see." She sounded a little disappointed. "Well that's okay! The time will come—I'm sure of it," said Sarah confidently.

"I hope you're right." Stephanie wondered what was holding John back, but she figured John just needed some time to decide to propose. "*We have plenty of time,*" she thought to herself, as she continued on with her day.

The clock chimed seven times. Stephanie looked up in a panic.

"Seven o'clock already? I'm going to be late! Where has the day gone?" she thought to herself as she rushed to put on her favorite red dress. The heavy pendulum swayed back and forth, filling the air with its monotonous sound.

Tick tock…tick tock…tick tock

She had just finished putting on her black heels when she heard John come through the front door.

"Coming!" she called out. She quickly rushed to grab her purse, then stepped into the living area. She found John sitting on the couch, dressed in a collared shirt and slacks.

"You look beautiful," sighed John. He stood and grabbed his keys. "Are you ready to go?"

"Absolutely!" she said.

Stephanie and John left the apartment, and John drove them to her favorite restaurant. After a wonderful dinner, John took Stephanie back to their apartment. They sat on the couch and stared into each other's eyes. All they saw was the love they had for each other.

"I really enjoyed our dinner tonight…" began John. He felt the sudden urge to bring up the possibility of marriage—everything had gone so well tonight, and it would be the perfect night to propose to Stephanie.

"I did too," she responded with a smile. She rubbed her temples, as if with discomfort.

"Everything okay?" asked John.

"Oh...yeah. Everything's fine—just a little headache," she responded. She looked up at John's face and smiled.

"Well you know, I was just thinking..." he began again.

"Yes?"

Then, the fear of rejection suddenly struck John again. What if she wasn't ready yet? He didn't want to propose to her until he was absolutely sure that was what she wanted.

"...do you want something to drink?" he finished quickly.

Stephanie was struck with disappointment. Silence filled the air for a moment, and the pendulum on the wall suddenly became a little too loud.

Tick tock...tick tock...tick tock

She had hoped that John had something more important to say. Her brow furrowed as she became suddenly more aware of the throbbing in her head. *"That darn headache,"* she thought to herself. Suddenly the only sound she could hear was the pendulum on the wall clock.

Tick tock...tick tock...tick tock

John's voice brought her back to the present. "Do you want something to drink, Stephanie?" he asked again.

"Yeah, sure, maybe some wine," she responded flatly. She rubbed her temples some more, hoping the headache would soon pass.

John stood up from the couch and went into the kitchen to pour some drinks. He opened a bottle of red wine, and poured a small amount into two wine glasses. *"Maybe I should just pop the question,"* he thought to himself. *"What if I lose her...but then again, what if she isn't ready?"* John was torn about what to do. He finished pouring the drinks, then returned to the living room. "I had this bottle of red wine that a friend gave to me—I've wanted to try it for a while, so here it is!" he said with a big smile as he entered the living room. He handed Stephanie a glass and sat beside her. Stephanie took a sip, then put her glass down on the coffee table. John moved closer to her and began kissing her. He reached for the zipper on the back of her dress, and passion ensued.

The clock chimed ten. The loud, clear tones exploded through the apartment.

DING...DING...DING

Stephanie's body went limp beneath him. John looked down at her, and his smile vanished. He felt he had been struck by something—his heart fell into an abyss, his stomach twisted. Time slowed, he froze, unable to move.

Stephanie was lying on the couch, her eyes rolled back, her body shaking as if she had been gripped by a seizure. John didn't know what to do—a million horrific thoughts flashed before his eyes as he lay beside her, jaw dropped, staring at Stephanie.

Then, suddenly, he came back to reality as his emergency training took hold. He jumped off the couch, knelt on the floor by Stephanie's side and tried to awaken her.

"Stephanie! Stephanie, wake up! Wake up, honey!" he yelled. She became stiff, unresponsive to all of John's words. John was in a state of panic. He stood up and grabbed his cell phone, and with fumbling hands, managed to dial 911.

"Harris County Police Department," said a calm voice on the telephone.

"I need an ambulance immediately my girlfriend is unconscious and she's not responding and she isn't waking up…I don't know what to do, we need help!" John was hyperventilating and in shock. He could barely form his sentences.

"We'll have an ambulance there as soon as possible. Can you tell me what happened, sir?"

"Yeah, I uh…I just found her here…on the couch," he said. He couldn't bring himself to say more about the events leading to Stephanie's current condition.

"Okay sir, try to remain calm."

Remaining calm was not really a choice. Stephanie was still unconscious as John hung up the phone. He ran back to her side. Her heart was still beating—she had a pulse, and he could tell she was still breathing, but she would not respond to him. John began to cry inexorably—he didn't know what to do.

"Please be okay, please please be okay..." he repeated relentlessly.

After about six minutes, two paramedics finally arrived. John quickly rose to let them in. A slender female dressed in a dark blue medic uniform came through the door first, followed by a similarly clothed husky man. Between them was a stretcher. They immediately rushed to Stephanie's side.

"Can you hear me ma'am? Can you tell me your name?" shouted the female medic.

Stephanie did not respond, and she had a very rigid, board-like neck. The paramedics noted that she was unconscious and unresponsive. A tube was put in Stephanie's throat to intubate her for air protection, and the two paramedics lifted her and put her on the stretcher.

"We'll need to take her to the hospital," said the man in an assertive voice.

"Oh—right, okay..." stammered John. His mind was still in shock. He followed the paramedics to the ambulance, where they lifted the stretcher with

Stephanie and put her in the ambulance. John followed—he didn't want to leave Stephanie's side. In the ambulance, the paramedics monitored Stephanie's blood pressure and put in an IV as she was rushed to the hospital.

10:30 PM—Bay City Hospital

In the emergency room of the nearest hospital, the ER doctor on call, Dr. Jones, was bustling back and forth between patients. It was an unusually busy day in the ER—there had been a major accident on the nearby highway, and numerous people with motor vehicle injuries needed treatment. Dr. Jones had been notified by the paramedics that another emergency case would arrive shortly. He hoped the case wasn't too serious—the ER was already packed.

Within ten minutes, the ambulance arrived. The two paramedics jumped out of the back, carrying a stretcher with a young woman on it. Behind them tailed a young man with hands tightly fisted at his sides and brow furrowed with concern.

"Must be the husband or boyfriend," thought Dr. Jones.

As the paramedics entered the hospital, Dr. Jones rushed to their side and listened attentively as the female paramedic began to update him on the woman's condition.

"We have a 27-year-old female, found

unconscious and unresponsive at the scene. She was found by her boyfriend on the couch. Intubated on the field, IV in right wrist. Blood pressure is 160/90 and exhibiting signs of tachycardia," shouted the paramedic as Stephanie was rushed in.

"Alright let's get a CT scan stat!" shouted Dr. Jones.

He put Stephanie on a respirator, and two nearby nurses grabbed Stephanie's gurney and transported her to the imaging area, where a CT scan was done. Stephanie remained unconscious. Dr. Jones looked at the scan, his eyes searching. The problem immediately caught his eyes. "*Oh no*," he thought to himself. "*This is not good…*"

"You'll have to stay in the waiting room now, sir," said a serious nurse with an authoritative voice.

John was furious—he was confused and did not know what was happening to Stephanie. He wanted to stay by her bedside, but they wouldn't let him. He felt he was in the dark. The nurse led him to a waiting room, where he paced anxiously. He couldn't sit still—thoughts of the possibility of Stephanie's death consumed him as he wondered what would happen to her. He wondered if she would ever wake up, if he could ever talk to her again. "*This can't be it…this wasn't supposed to be the end…we were supposed to have so much more time…*" he thought furiously. He continued to pace, back and forth, when the ER physician walked in.

"I'm Dr. Jones—you came in with Stephanie, right?" asked the physician as he walked towards John.

John immediately rushed to the physician. "Yeah I'm with Stephanie...I'm John—is she going to be okay? What's wrong with her?" he quickly asked.

"Well, Stephanie's CT scans show that she suffered catastrophic bleeding in her brain. She had a subarachnoid hemorrhage, meaning there is blood in her subarachnoid space, which is between the brain and the skull."

"What?! Oh my god..." John's hands rose to his head in shock. "Is that... is that treatable? Is she going to be okay? What do we do now?"

"We'll need to transfer Stephanie to the medical center so she can be under the care of a neurosurgeon."

John's heart sank. "*A neurosurgeon?*" The ER physician had avoided answering John's questions about whether or not Stephanie was going to be okay, and that worried John.

"Is she going to be okay though? You didn't answer my question," he repeated.

"I'm sorry sir, but you will have to wait for the neurosurgeon's opinion. For now, Stephanie is on a ventilator," replied Dr. Jones. "We will start her transfer immediately."

John felt nauseous. A million questions were

racing through his mind, all without answers. His future with Stephanie looked bleak. "*God, I hope the neurosurgeon can help Stephanie...oh please,*" he thought over and over again.

CHAPTER TWO

Dr. Bindal was awoken by the blaring sound of his ringing telephone. He opened his eyes and squinted as he looked at the clock. It was just after midnight. Being on call had its drawbacks, and the lack of sleep was one of them.

He fumbled in the dark for the phone receiver, and sleepily held it up to his head. "This is Dr. Bindal," he said into his phone with traces of a yawn muffling his voice.

"Hi Dr. Bindal. This is Dr. Jones. I have a patient here with a ruptured aneurysm and I need a neurosurgeon to take care of her. I'm having her transferred to your ICU right now," said a deep voice on the other line. "I've given her some medications to keep her blood pressure down." With an aneurysm, the chance of re-rupturing is extremely high. Patients with ruptured aneurysms are often given medication to lower their blood pressure to decrease the chance

78

of the aneurysm rupturing again.

"Alright. Thanks, Dr. Jones. I'll be there shortly," he said, putting down the phone. Dr. Bindal's wife turned in the bed, awoken by the phone call.

"What's going on?" she asked sleepily.

"I have to go to the hospital now—there's an emergency."

"Now?" she said, looking at the window. The weather had taken a drastic turn—it was a chilly, stormy night. "It can't wait till the morning? The weather looks terrible."

"No, I have to go now." As painful as it was to leave the comfort of his home and bed in the middle of the night, he knew a patient's life likely depended on his presence.

"Okay, just be careful," she said, falling back asleep.

Dr. Bindal stood quickly from the bed and changed his clothes into scrubs, then rushed down to his car. He drove through the heavy rain towards the hospital.

Ruptured aneurysms were dangerous—the majority of people who have a rupture die on the spot. For those whose aneurysm bleeds in a small, controlled manner and then quickly seals itself, significant impairment is almost guaranteed and the majority of these patients die in the hospital or go into an irreversible vegetative state. Stephanie was lucky—the initial rupture did not kill her and she made it to the hospital and was still alive, but her situation was very grave, and Dr. Bindal knew that.

When he arrived, he immediately made his way to the ICU. On the way to Stephanie's bedside, he passed by the private waiting room where he saw a young man nervously pacing. The man—with tearful concern in his eyes—looked up at Dr. Bindal as he passed, and for a brief moment, their eyes met. "*Poor man*," thought Dr. Bindal, as he wondered what was causing this man's grief, unknowing that the stranger's fate was very much entwined with his own.

When he arrived in the ICU, Dr. Bindal first reviewed Stephanie's CT scan and tested her neurologic function. Stephanie was very drowsy and did not follow commands. She localized to stimulation, meaning when pinched, she would respond by moving her hand to where she was pinched. She moved all of her extremities, but her eyes were closed and she was still intubated. Her condition suggested the earliest stages of a coma.

"We need to get a four-vessel cerebral angiogram," he said to the nurse. Dr. Bindal then paused for a moment—he had a decision to make which would determine whether Stephanie would live or die. Stephanie had hydrocephalus, or a buildup of cerebrospinal fluid in her brain, and Dr. Bindal had to decide whether to put a drain in now or later. The bleeding from her aneurysm had interfered with the absorption of the cerebrospinal fluid, and her intracranial pressure was extremely high. If the drain is put in now, however, then Stephanie's intracranial pressure could drop dramatically, causing her aneurysm to re-rupture. However, if the drain isn't put in, then Stephanie's condition could deteriorate further.

Dr. Bindal thought carefully, analyzing the pros and cons of each of his two choices. Then, he made a decision.

"I'm going to refrain from putting in the drain," he said to the attending nurse. "Let's get that angiogram so we can locate her aneurysm."

The nurse nodded, and Stephanie was transported on a gurney to the radiology floor, where she was taken to the angiography suite. The angiography suite was a spacious room with large medical equipment. The fluoroscopic equipment and monitors were huge and overbearing, and the light from the ceiling glittered on the crisp white of the machines.

The radiologist prepared Stephanie's upper thigh area near her groin and inserted a long needle into her femoral artery. A guide wire was threaded through the needle and into her artery, and then a catheter was put in over the wire. The radiologist squirted angiography dye, then used fluoroscopy to determine the location of the guide wire in Stephanie's body. He followed the guide wire up the aorta, through the subclavian arteries, and finally into her carotid arteries, which supply Stephanie's brain with oxygenated blood. The radiologist was careful— he risked tearing any one of Stephanie's major arteries with the guide wire, causing further damage to Stephanie's already perilous state.

Once the guide wire was in Stephanie's carotid arteries, the radiologist injected a dye which would flow through all of the arteries in the brain that are fed by the artery in which the wire had been placed. Any aneurysm along an artery would fill with the dye and could then be seen on the angiogram as a little "blob". Radiologists have multiple goals in mind when performing angiograms. The location of the aneurysm must be found, and any vasospasm should be established. In addition, the unique anatomy of the patient's Circle of Willis must be determined, since every person's Circle of Willis is different and the differences can heavily influence how a surgery is approached and done.

When the angiogram was finished, the radiologist called Stephanie's neurosurgeon to give his report.

"Hi Dr. Bindal, this is Dr. Lawrence. I have the report of the angiogram on your ruptured aneurysm patient," he said into the phone after connecting with Dr. Bindal.

"Hey Dr. Lawrence. So, what do we have here?" asked Dr. Bindal.

"Well it looks like you have a 7-mm left carotid ophthalmic aneurysm. You don't have good cross filling from the right side, precluding your option of occluding the left carotid artery. The rest of the vessels are clear."

"Okay thanks Dr. Lawrence." Dr. Bindal put down his phone. Aneurysm cases were difficult as they were, but a carotid ophthalmic aneurysm was exceptionally risky. He called for an operating room immediately, telling them to set up for an aneurysm clipping craniotomy. Then, he went to the waiting room to meet with any family that Stephanie may have.

John was still pacing, back and forth, his brows furrowed, his hands tense. He was waiting for the doctor to come talk to him about Stephanie. It was all so unexpected—her sudden slip out of consciousness, the rush to the ER. They had been having such a wonderful night. John could never have guessed that everything would come to an end so quickly. He thought they had more time.

Time. The age-old paradox. When we desire less, it moves slowly, undulating at a snail's pace, and yet when we feel we have enough, it quickens, and moments become fleeting. "*This can't be it*," he thought to himself. "*Oh God please help Stephanie*."

John was tired—it was five o'clock in the morning and he hadn't slept an ounce. His eyes were red and puffy, his hair disheveled. He felt worn, torn, and completely powerless.

The doors to the waiting room swung open, and a large man dressed in scrubs with big glasses approached John. The man's comforting face was accompanied by a commanding presence that called for immediacy and attention.

"Hi John, I'm Dr. Bindal. Is there anyone else here with Stephanie?" asked the doctor.

"No…Stephanie doesn't have any family here. I'm the only one here for her." John paused. He could read in the doctor's face that the news would not be too good. "Is she going to be okay?"

"Well John, as the ER doctor may have told you, Stephanie had a ruptured carotid ophthalmic aneurysm. This is a very dangerous situation—"

"What does that mean exactly…an aneurysm I mean," interrupted John. He was tired of hearing medical terms that meant nothing to him. He just wanted to understand what was happening to Stephanie.

"It means that there is weakness in the wall of an artery in Stephanie's brain, which causes an abnormal widening. The widened area, or the aneurysm, ruptured. In Stephanie's case, the aneurysm ruptured and then resealed itself, which is why she is alive right now. However, the aneurysm can rupture again at any time, resulting in death. It could rupture right now, and she could die, and I wouldn't be able to stop it," explained Dr. Bindal.

"So there's nothing you can do? There's no way to treat her?" John exclaimed. "But she's so healthy…she always has been! I just don't understand how this happened! I mean, she had been having some headaches more recently but that's it! She was perfectly fine…"

"The headaches were most likely warning bleeds. That happens sometimes when someone has an aneurysm."

"So I should have brought her in earlier, then?!" John's stomach twisted. "*It's all my fault*," he thought to himself.

"Let's not talk about that, John. Let's talk about where we are now," replied Dr. Bindal gently.

"Why did this happen though?" asked John.

"Well, we don't know why aneurysms rupture. Sometimes heavy lifting that results in increased blood pressure can make it happen. In some instances, sexual intercourse can make an aneurysm rupture."

John's face darkened.

"Was she doing something in particular when this happened?" asked the doctor.

"Um...no she was just lying on the sofa," replied John. He didn't know why he lied. "So, what happens now?"

The doctor continued in a calm and gentle voice. "Stephanie has hydrocephalus now, and the pressure in her brain can rise and take her life. I can't put a shunt in at this time, because the shunt would clog up from the blood, so I'm going to have to put in a drain that externally drains the fluid until the cerebrospinal fluid clears.

"Now, clipping the aneurysm is the only way to prevent re-rupture and death. Coiling the aneurysm is not an option, since the aneurysm has a broad neck and its location next to the optic nerve makes it dangerous to coil. This is a very high risk operation, because the aneurysm can re-rupture prior to me getting it exposed, or while I am exposing it, and if I am unable to control the bleeding, it means death. Stephanie's brain is very stiff right now and there are blood clots all over the place, and the anatomy is sometimes difficult to navigate, which could also result in injury to cranial nerves, stroke, and death.

"The clipping may not go well, and it could occlude her carotid artery, in which case she'll end up with a massive left sided stroke, and since she's right handed, she would lose her ability for speech. Even then, it is highly possible she may not make a meaningful recovery given her current neurologic status, despite successful surgery.

"The final point is that she will suffer from vasospasm, which occurs after the surgery. Vasospasm causes the blood vessels to clamp down which can result in serious strokes, loss of function, and death, despite successful surgery. Her risk for vasospasm can exist up to three weeks after the bleed, so she will be in the ICU for a long time in critical condition. She'll need to be in the ICU for vasospasm and for the hydrocephalus because of the drain. Once the cerebrospinal fluid clears up and the vasospasm resolves, we can switch her to a permanent shunt." Dr. Bindal paused for a moment, collecting his thoughts.

"Right now, we are keeping her blood pressure really low to prevent re-bleeding, but when vasospasm strikes, we will need to raise her blood pressure to maximize blood flow to the brain. That's why we need to clip the aneurysm now, so that the risk of re-bleeding when we raise the blood pressure is reduced," finished Dr. Bindal. He had been completely honest with John, imparting on him every possible turn that Stephanie's condition could take.

John sobbed inexorably, devastated with the news. The doctor had uttered the word "death" countless times, and John could not stand the thought of losing Stephanie. He shook his head with disbelief. Everything felt so surreal to him. "*I should have proposed…*" he thought to himself repeatedly. "*Oh God, why did I not marry her.*"

Dr. Bindal sensed terror, disbelief, and grief surfacing in John's expression.

"Please save her, Dr. Bindal. Please save Stephanie," implored John as he placed his hands on the doctor's shoulders. Dr. Bindal sighed as he looked at John's face, which had an expression that doctors often saw from patient's families in grave situations such as these. John looked at him as if he were the only person standing between him and death and despair. It was the look of a desperate family member, looking at a doctor as the only chance for survival. It was the look of desolation, of imploration, where there isn't a chance for a second opinion. In the midst of the night with an emergency case, the doctor you get is your only chance. It is one of the few times in life when a man looks at another man as his only chance for salvation.

Dr. Bindal nodded. He understood John's frenzied state. "I'll do my best John," he said in an attempt to comfort him, though he wasn't sure that was possible. He left the waiting room for the operating room, where the preparations for the surgery had already begun.

The operating room was bustling with quiet activity. Nurses were setting up the instrument tables and preparing the room for surgery. Dr. Bindal entered the room and addressed the operating team, his voice surging through the room as the only source of noise and the single source of command.

"I need two scrub techs and two circulators," he said with authority. A ruptured aneurysm case like this is tricky, and the more hands that are available, the better it is.

He turned to the scrub nurse setting up the instrument table and said, "Everything has to be ready prior to the patient's arrival. Get the microscope draped, get the aneurysm clips laid out and preselected. I need three temporary clips loaded and I want a 7-mm angle oblique Yasargil aneurysm clip."

The nurse nodded as she mentally noted the doctor's wishes. She always wondered how he knew what aneurysm clip he would need, but she never questioned him.

Before the microscope was draped, Dr. Bindal adjusted it to ensure proper optic set-up. Then, he turned to the circulating nurse who was running in and out of the operating room, bringing in needed supplies.

"Get me 4 units packed RBC."

"4 units, Dr. Bindal?" asked the nurse. Four units of blood seemed excessive, so she wanted to confirm that the doctor meant what he said. Only for neurosurgery does the blood bank release so much blood without any blood loss having occurred yet.

"Yes, we need it in the room in case the aneurysm ruptures. If it ruptures, there will be no time to look for it. We need to be prepared for all the possibilities," he replied. "Prepare my chair, headlight, and cooling vest. Get the Midas-Rex drill and get an acorn M3, B1 side cutting drill bit, the AM8, and the AM8 diamond."

"Diamond?" asked the nurse, confirming the doctor's orders.

"Yes, the diamond drill bit is used around the most sensitive neural structures to give a very controlled drilling of bone," he replied. Dr. Bindal paused, collecting his thoughts, recalling with detail each item that was distinctly necessary for this operation.

"Have three sucker tips ready instead of the usual two...just in case," he added.

As preparations continued, Stephanie was

wheeled in on a gurney by the circulating nurse and the transport team. The anesthesiologist came with them and was "bagging" Stephanie, providing artificial ventilation with a respirator bag.

Upon Stephanie's arrival, the entire operating room erupted with noise. A multitude of monitoring devices came with Stephanie, all producing different tones of sound. The heart rate monitor began to beep with each beat of Stephanie's heart.

Tha dump...tha dump...tha dump

Beep beep...beep beep...beep beep

Tick tock...tick tock...tick tock

The operating team made noise, yelling commands at each other as preparations ensued. Dr. Bindal stood and watched as the fanfare persisted, his own heart rate elevating as his time to perform came near. Stephanie was transferred from the gurney to the operating room bed with all of the equipment. Once the transfer was complete, the anesthesiologist, scrub nurses, circulating nurses, and the anesthesia technicians all worked to prepare her for surgery, placing stockings, compression boots, arterial and central lines, and all other necessary components of surgery.

About thirty minutes later, the initial preparations were complete. Stephanie was placed in the special carbon fiber, radiolucent Mayfield head holder (a three-point fixation device designed for intraoperative angiography) so that her head could be positioned for optimal approach to the aneurysm. Dr.

Bindal mentally visualized the three-dimensional location of Stephanie's aneurysm and determined how to tilt and rotate her head to the proper angle.

"Raise her back 10 degrees," said Dr. Bindal. The anesthesia technicians raised Stephanie's back ten degrees as per Dr. Bindal's request, allowing for venous drainage and bleed reduction.

The time had come for the operation to begin. Dr. Bindal turned to the anesthesiologist and asked, "What is the patient's blood pressure?"

"120/80," responded the anesthesiologist.

"You need Nipride to lower her blood pressure down below 90/60, and pressers to raise the blood pressure over 180 systolic. You need to do that within a matter of minutes of my command. Are you familiar with the dosing for cerebral protection?"

"Yes."

"That's what you need to be prepared, including an etomidate drip. I want one gram of Dilantin, 10 mg of Decadron, and 1 gram of Ancef now, and then 50 grams of Mannitol when I make my incision to reduce the swelling in the brain. I also need the patient to be hyperventilated to an end-tidal pCO_2 of 25."

The anesthesiologist nodded and then placed a warmer on Stephanie to keep her warm during the operation. Just as he was about to flip the switch to turn on the warmer, Dr. Bindal cut in.

"Don't turn it on. Let the patient stay cold for cerebral protection. At the conclusion of the case, you can warm the patient."

It was seven o'clock in the morning now, and Stephanie was finally ready for surgery.

Dr. Bindal shaved her head to prepare for the craniotomy and for the intraventricular catheter (IVC). Her head and the left side of her neck were prepped, as well as her groin around the retained femoral catheter from the angiogram. Dr. Bindal marked the prospective incision and draped Stephanie's neck and head. He infiltrated the marking with lidocaine without epinephrine to ensure her blood pressure does not rise, which could cause a premature rupture. Dr. Bindal then stepped back and looked down at Stephanie's neck.

"Ten blade," he said to the scrub nurse, his right hand outstretched.

Dr. Bindal stood at the head of the operating table with the scalpel in his right hand, looking down at Stephanie's head, his headlight shining on her shaved scalp. He inhaled deeply, focusing, as he brought the scalpel down on the left side of Stephanie's neck, making the first incision.

CHAPTER THREE

Guilt is a terrible thing. It consumes us, feeding off our darkest fears and thoughts, all hidden in our subconscious. John felt guilty. He feared he had cursed his time with Stephanie, as if his hesitance in proposing to her had brought this upon her. "*The doctor said Stephanie had warning bleeds,*" John thought to himself. "*I should have noticed it...*" Thoughts of Stephanie's death continued to churn in his head. Stephanie was perfect for him, and now he may never be able to speak to her again. "*Please God, please save her. I'm going to marry her. I'm going to make this right.*"

John paced back and forth in the waiting area, rubbing his temples and running his hands through his hair. Time passed, and he decided to sit down. Physicians of all kinds walked in and out of the waiting room area, addressing the family members of different patients. John watched as many family members broke into smiles, thanking God and shaking hands with their doctors fervently, while the faces of others turned dark with denial, confusion, and anguish.

He continued to wait endless hours. His faith dwindled, but he held hope that the doctor could save Stephanie.

CHAPTER FOUR

As the first incision was made, the skin flap in Stephanie's neck bled profusely. Dr. Bindal applied cautery to control the bleeding. He then placed retractors, providing exposure to the internal anatomy of the neck. With careful dissection of the fascial planes, the internal and external carotid arteries in Stephanie's neck were now exposed. The vessels glistened red against the white surrounding tissue, pumping blood to Stephanie's head and brain. Dr. Bindal placed vessel loops around the arteries to gain proximal control of blood flow in the event the aneurysm starts bleeding.

"So why did we open the neck first?" asked the scrub nurse.

"We need to be able to control blood flow to the aneurysm. This aneurysm is right at the base of the skull. In order to control the carotid artery on both sides of the aneurysm, we have to expose the carotid artery in the neck," explained Dr. Bindal.

He moved to the head, where he made a small incision on the right paramedian frontal region down to the skull. He used the drill to create a hole in the skull to the dura, which is the lining of the brain. He then made a small opening in the dura and cauterized any blood vessels at the surface that bled as a result. He made an incision in the surface of the brain with a sharp knife. "*Time to place the ventricular catheter*," he thought to himself, as a three-dimensional picture of Stephanie's brain formed in his head. He imagined the exact position of the fluid filled cavities in her brain as he planned the insertion of the intraventricular catheter (IVC).

After a few moments, Dr. Bindal selected an angle of approach and inserted the catheter into Stephanie's brain, hoping his calculations were correct and the catheter would pierce the ventricle with a single shot so as to avoid neurologic injury. As he inserted the catheter, he felt a small resistance and a pop, indicating that he had successfully entered the lateral ventricle in the brain. He removed the guide wire and bloody cerebrospinal fluid immediately came squirting out of the end of the catheter, relieving some of the pressure that had built up. Dr. Bindal quickly controlled the release of the fluid to avoid a sudden drop in intracranial pressure, which could potentially trigger a re-rupture of the aneurysm in Stephanie's brain.

After attaching the catheter to a drainage bag to secure it, Dr. Bindal ensured Stephanie's blood pressure was low to avoid rupturing the aneurysm again.

A craniotomy was then performed on the left side of the head.

"Let's get the chair and operating microscope into position," he said. The circulating nurse, a genial, middle-aged gentleman, immediately moved to bring the chair into position. Dr. Bindal and the scrub nurse together rotated the giant, overhanging microscope into place just above Stephanie's head.

"Lights off. Quiet everybody," commanded Dr. Bindal to the operating room staff. He incised the dura and turned the dural flap, using retractor blades to retract the frontal and temporal lobes of Stephanie's brain. He coagulated and divided the sphenoparietal veins with the bipolar cautery and opened the optic cistern, revealing thick, gooey blood clots filling the space. Dr. Bindal suctioned out the blood clots along with the cerebrospinal fluid. Because of the initial rupture of the aneurysm, Stephanie's brain was stiff—it lacked its usual spongy, soft appearance. The normal anatomy of her brain was obliterated, and exposure was difficult. Dr. Bindal incised the arachnoid of the carotid cistern, exposing the optic nerve and carotid artery. He then performed a clinoidectomy, helping to gain better access to the aneurysm. He incised the distal dural ring, finally reaching the depths of Stephanie's brain in which the aneurysm lay.

1990—Mayfield Clinic, Cincinnati, Ohio

"Dr. Bindal, Dr. Levi—I want you two down in the rat lab today," said Dr. Tew, chairman of the neurosurgery department, in his husky, commanding voice.

"The rat lab? What are we going to do down there…?" inquired Dr. Bindal. Dr. Tew ignored the question and began to lead Dr. Bindal and Dr. Levi towards the rat laboratory on the hospital campus.

"I hope he remembers we're interns, not lab scientists…" chuckled Dr. Levi as he and Dr. Bindal followed Dr. Tew along the unfamiliar path.

Dr. Tew led them down to the basement of the hospital, through dark corridors lined with brick walls. They arrived at two double doors, large and gloomy in appearance. Inside, research scientists were bustling about conducting experiments. Dr. Tew moved towards a dark, granite laboratory bench upon which lay cages full of small, white mice. The mice were scurrying about in the cage, squeaking and squealing, unaware of their unfortunate fates.

Dr. Bindal remembered a time back in high school when he conducted research in a lab that was isolating proteins from rat livers. The rats had to be killed for the research, and he was given the task of killing them. He would take the rat's head and body, then stretch it, essentially hanging the creature. He remembered how easy it was to kill them, and the remorse he felt afterwards. He had vowed never to participate in that kind of research again.

"Here are the mice," said Dr. Tew as he wore gloves. He opened one of the cages and picked up a mouse by its tail. He placed it on the counter top, anesthetized it, then cut open its neck and severed the carotid artery. The mouse began to bleed profusely. Dr. Tew turned looked up at his residents.

"Today, you will train in microsurgery. Developing your microsurgical techniques is important for being a good neurosurgeon," he said. "Ajay, grab some gloves and a suture kit, and sew this mouse's carotid artery back together."

Dr. Bindal stood frozen as the mouse bled.

"You better be quick. This mouse is dying."

Without any choice, Dr. Bindal grabbed some gloves and sutures. The task proved extremely difficult. The vessels were so tiny, nearly invisible. His hands were shaking, adrenaline rushing through his body. Never before had he worked with such small sutures under such high magnification. It seemed impossible to sew the vessel back together. Time was ticking, and minutes later, the mouse died.

Dr. Levi watched in horror. "How exactly is this going to help us with our surgical technique?" he exclaimed.

"The mice have tiny vessels—much smaller than the blood vessels in humans, so you will be building your microsurgical techniques. You'll have to use the highest magnification on the microscope and the smallest sutures. Take another mouse, cut its carotid artery, then see if you can sew it back together again. If the mouse lives, you were successful. If not, well...keep trying. You can practice with as many mice as you want. Once you are successful with the carotid, you can move on to the femoral, and so on," stated Dr. Tew in a matter-of-fact voice.

Dr. Bindal shook his head. The mice were living, breathing creatures too. He was here to save lives, not take them. Despite these feelings, he had his orders.

He took another mouse, anesthetized it, and carefully began to cut the carotid artery. As soon as the artery was snipped, he quickly tried to sew it back together. He was not nearly quick enough, not nearly nimble enough with the sutures. The second mouse died, and so did five others. The process was taxing. With each mouse's death, Dr. Bindal felt emotionally drained and defeated. He wanted so badly to save just one mouse, as though to vindicate himself for the death of the others.

He continued to practice until finally, with a stroke of luck and his newfound skills, he managed his first success. A single mouse finally survived the operation. Two subsequent mice joined the ranks of the first survivor, and Dr. Bindal felt an immense pride and relief. At the end of the day, he had managed to save three mice out of ten. He placed the three surviving mice back in their cage for recovery. He looked over to Dr. Levi, who had just finished his last attempt at saving a mouse.

"Did you get any survivals?" asked Dr. Bindal.

"Just two. You?"

"I saved three."

Dr. Levi nodded. The survival rate was not too great, but the skills they had gained did seem useful for future surgeries.

The next day, when Dr. Bindal arrived at the hospital, he decided to stop by the rat lab first before going on his rounds. *"Maybe I'll just check to see how the mice are recovering,"* he thought to himself as he walked towards Dr. Tew to check-in for the day.

"Good morning, Dr. Tew," he said. "Is it okay if I see the mice that survived from yesterday before I go on my rounds? I'm curious to see how they are."

"Oh, the mice you were working on? They euthanized them last night," responded Dr. Tew in a casual voice.

"What? Why would they do that? I spent hours yesterday trying to save them!" Dr. Bindal felt furious. He couldn't explain the emotional attachment he felt to the mice. It didn't seem fair that they had to die anyways. "I didn't want them to die. I worked hard to save their lives."

"Dr. Bindal, those mice served their purpose," said Dr. Tew.

"And what purpose is that exactly?" he asked defiantly.

"One day, the skills you learned while operating on those mice will save a person's life. You'll have to do a craniotomy one day—say, an aneurysm clipping, for example. It may require deft microsurgical techniques. When that patient lives, he or she will have those mice to thank for it."

The aneurysm had an ominous appearance. A red bulge in the vessel wall, it pulsed with every beat of Stephanie's heart. Like a balloon filling increasingly, the aneurysm was testing the strength of the arterial walls and approaching a rupture point again. It was a bomb ready to explode. Ten percent of the entire heart's output gushed through the vessel and poured into the aneurysm. A rupture would cause loss of this significant amount of blood—a loss too great to survive.

Dr. Bindal had to move quickly. The aneurysm was delicate. He cleared the carotid artery distal to the aneurysm, removing all blood clots and clearing out an area for placement of a distal clip to prevent the backflow of blood. This way, if a rupture does occur, blood will not flow forward and backwards through the artery. However, a third pathway for the blood flow from the aneurysm still remained—the ophthalmic artery.

Tick tock...tick tock...tick tock

The continuous sounds of the machines monitoring Stephanie persisted in clock-like rhythm. Difficult to expose, the ophthalmic artery was the last location a clip had to be placed before Dr. Bindal could be assured that a rupture would not cause major damage to Stephanie's brain. He began to dissect around the aneurysm. Thinly walled, the aneurysm had a large, dark red clot over it—the location of the initial rupture. Stephanie's brain was extremely rigid. It was clear that damage had already been done. As Dr. Bindal peered through the microscope and into Stephanie's brain, he noticed that the aneurysm pressed against her optic nerve. "*Strange*," he thought to himself. "*I wonder if she had some vision problems prior to the rupture.*"

Dr. Bindal continued to dissect around the aneurysm. The operating room was silent. Everyone had turned their attention to the large television screen displaying the image Dr. Bindal was seeing through the microscope. With deft motions of his nimble fingers, he dissected slowly, carefully. Blood pumped through the aneurysm as it throbbed in precise synchrony with the heart, when all of a sudden, despite all measures, the aneurysm burst.

CHAPTER FIVE

Time slowed. It was an explosion. Blood gushed through the millimeter-wide opening through which Dr. Bindal was looking. His view through the microscope was obliterated. It was red everywhere—blood filled the opening continuously with each beat of Stephanie's heart. Dr. Bindal's heart fell through his chest—his hands froze momentarily. The nurses and operating room staff stood, staring at the television screen, eyes frozen, mouths gaping. Suddenly, a powerful voice brought them back to reality.

"Drop the blood pressure!" commanded Dr. Bindal. His heart rate and blood pressure rose. He had been trained to handle situations like this. Now, more than ever, his steady hands and expertise knowledge were crucial. There was no room for mistakes now.

"Cottonoid," he said quickly to the scrub nurse.

He applied cottonoid directly to the aneurysm, hoping that the added pressure may reduce the bleeding.

It was not enough. Blood continued to gush through the vessel wall, instantaneously filling the small opening in which Dr. Bindal was working. The nurses were in a state of panic and were grabbing blood and fluids as Dr. Bindal worked deftly to control the situation. Two suction devices failed, and the third emergency device had to be used.

"Temporary clip." He reached over to the incision he made in the neck and placed a temporary clip to gain proximal control of the carotid artery. He returned to the operative scene, and applied cottonoid to the aneurysm again, momentarily allowing some visualization of the distal aspect of the carotid artery.

"Another temporary clip."

The scrub nurse quickly handed him a second temporary clip, which he applied to the distal aspect of the carotid artery, now trapping some of the blood flow. The leakage of blood was now reduced, though it was not eliminated.

Half of Stephanie's brain was now lacking blood. Protecting it was vital, or severe repercussions could ensue. With Stephanie's life on the line, Dr. Bindal turned to the anesthesiologist and instructed him in an assertive voice. "Institute etomidate," said Dr. Bindal. "Raise the blood pressure quickly to 180 systolic. We need to maximize blood flow from the right carotid and from the external carotid artery to the left cerebral hemisphere." He turned to the scrub nurse again. "Permanent clip."

"How long can she survive without blood flow to the brain?" asked the scrub nurse.

"You can't consciously hold your breath for more than two minutes. Brain damage will ensue after five to ten minutes."

The scrub nurse nervously handed Dr. Bindal the pre-selected permanent clip. Using his innate memory of the anatomy of the brain and his knowledge of neurosurgery, Dr. Bindal lowered the permanent clip into the pool of blood filling the opening, sliding the clip over where he believed lay the neck of the aneurysm. His movements were calculated carefully. Precision was necessary, and he could not miss. He had to avoid tearing the carotid artery as well as the ophthalmic artery to spare Stephanie's vision. The clip also had to be placed in a manner such that the optic nerve is not impinged.

"Call angiogram," said Dr. Bindal to the nearby circulating nurse. The nurse swiftly picked up the telephone receiver mounted on the operating room wall, calling for the angiographer. "We are going to shoot an angiogram to see if the carotid artery is intact and the aneurysm is obliterated. We also want to ensure the ophthalmic artery is patent." The nurse nodded as he repeated the information to the angiographer.

Dr. Bindal turned to the scrub nurses to his right. "Temporary clip applier," he said with an outstretched hand. The nurse handed him the temporary clip applier, and Dr. Bindal began to release the temporary clips that he had previously placed. He released the distal temporary clip first to see if any bleeding was present from the aneurysm.

"No bleeding," he said with a sigh of relief. He released the proximal clip next, and again, the aneurysm did not refill and did not bleed.

After a few moments, the angiographer arrived. With him, he brought the C-arm, a portable fluoroscopy device. Stephanie's brain was covered with wet towels and sponges, and the retractors were removed. The angiographer quickly passed his angiographic catheter into the left carotid artery. Within ten minutes, he reported to Dr. Bindal with his results.

"You have a successfully clipped aneurysm, and you preserved patent carotid and ophthalmic arteries," said the angiographer.

"Do I need to reposition the clip?" asked Dr. Bindal.

"Nope. It looks like your clipping is perfect."

Behind his mask, Dr. Bindal broke into a momentary smile. "Great," he said out loud to his operating room staff. "First shot perfect."

"What if the carotid artery was not patent? It's been thirty minutes. Would she have survived having her carotid artery occluded for thirty minutes?" asked the scrub nurse.

"With everything we've done, including the etomidate and blood pressure manipulation, carotid artery occlusion for thirty minutes can be tolerated," he responded with a wink. "Etomidate is a barbiturate that is short-acting and reduces the metabolism of neurons so they can tolerate low oxygen longer, and increasing blood pressure allows for blood flow from other vessels to the part of the brain where blood flow is compromised."

Dr. Bindal turned to the anesthesiologist. "Stop the etomidate and let her blood pressure return to normal," he said. He inspected the area of operation again, ensuring that all the bleeding was controlled. He squirted papaverine around the artery to reduce vasospasm in the vessel.

"So why do you squirt the papaverine on the blood vessels?" asked the scrub nurse.

"Papaverine dilates the blood vessels. When there is bleeding in the brain, the blood vessels are very sensitive and tend to constrict further. The papaverine will counteract that."

"Alright," he said to his nurses. "Time to close up." He closed the dura, re-attached the skull flap to the skull using plates, and attached the muscle and skin together. As the operation came to a close, the radiologist pulled the catheter out of the groin. A dressing was placed on the head and on the neck.

Stephanie was taken to the ICU, where a medical team was waiting to manage her ventilator. She had relief of her hydrocephalus, and the clipping of her aneurysm had been successful. Dr. Bindal re-examined Stephanie and found that her neurologic condition had improved significantly. Though she was still quite lethargic, Stephanie was not comatose and could follow commands and move all of her extremities.

Dr. Bindal breathed out a sigh of relief. The surgery had gone well, but Stephanie was not completely out of danger quite yet. She was at high risk of vasospasm (and subsequent stroke), and he would have to take measures to reduce that likelihood.

CHAPTER SIX

Six hours later, John was still in the waiting room when Dr. Bindal suddenly walked in. John stood quickly from his chair and walked towards the doctor.

"The surgery went well. Stephanie is waking up now and is showing improvement in her neurologic condition. We had the aneurysm rupture during the surgery, but I managed to get it under control," said Dr. Bindal.

"Dr. Bindal, thank you so much!" John exclaimed. He felt immediately elated. The torture of waiting had finally come to an end.

"John, it is important for you to understand that Stephanie's condition remains critical. With a ruptured aneurysm, patients can suffer from vasospasm—a reaction to subarachnoid hemorrhage. The blood vessels to Stephanie's brain will constrict and may cause a stroke, which can result in significant neurologic deficit or even death," explained Dr.

Bindal. "If this happens, the only way we can get more blood through her arteries is by maximizing her blood pressure and maximizing her heart's ability to push blood volume through the constricted vessels. If this fails, and it often does, Stephanie will suffer irreversible strokes."

John nodded slowly. Part of his relief had faded upon hearing the doctor's words. His only solace was in hoping that the success of the surgery would endure.

Postoperative Day #3

Sunlight poured through the hospital windows and fell gently on Stephanie's bed. She opened her eyes and found John sitting beside her, his hand resting on hers.

"Good morning," he said to her, smiling softly. Stephanie smiled back at him. "How are you feeling?" he asked.

"Better than before," she chuckled as she clasped his hand tightly.

"I love you," said John abruptly. He watched Stephanie intently for her reply. For a moment, Stephanie's mouth opened as if to respond when suddenly, her mouth closed and her body began to appear lethargic. She released her clutch on John's hand as the right side of her body became weak.

"Stephanie! Stephanie—wake up!" yelled

John. He quickly called for a nurse, who immediately paged the doctor.

Dr. Bindal entered the room moments later and swiftly examined Stephanie. He recognized Stephanie's symptoms as characteristic of vasospasm.

"Let's begin triple H therapy. Get her blood pressure up and her hemoglobin/hematocrit down to 10/30. Give her albumin/salt/fluid overload as well to hemodilute her. We need to get her heart pumping faster," said Dr. Bindal.

He consulted a cardiologist to place a Swan-Ganz Catheter directly into Stephanie's heart to help measure her heart output.

"We need to maximize her cardiac output and put her into as close to heart failure as possible," he explained to John.

"What? Why...I don't understand..." stammered John. The thought of Stephanie being near heart failure was far from comforting.

"This is one of those rare situations in medicine where we need to put Stephanie's body out of balance to protect her brain," the doctor explained.

After the triple H therapy was implemented, Stephanie's weakness suddenly disappeared. The symptoms of stroke had vanished, and John became hopeful again.

Postoperative Day #4

Despite all measures to maintain blood flow to her brain, Stephanie became symptomatic from vasospasm and began to show signs of stroke again. Dr. Bindal rushed into her room.

He pinched both of her arms—the left arm moved, but the right arm did not. Her level of consciousness had decreased, and her right sided weakness ensued.

"Let's intubate her," he commanded. He went out to talk to John.

"Look John, we are maxed out on the treatment, and Stephanie is still suffering neurologic deficit. This could result in permanent stroke, possibly even death," he said. "I'm sorry."

John became terrified. His lips trembled hearing the news. He shared the story of his love for Stephanie with the doctor.

John begged repeatedly, "Please Dr. Bindal, please do everything you can to save Stephanie. I should have married her. You are my witness—dear God, please save Stephanie. If Stephanie can survive this ordeal, I will marry her, no matter what."

Dr. Bindal felt sorry for John. After carefully thinking about options for Stephanie, he offered John one last hope for Stephanie.

"Well, we can try the papaverine injection—we can try it intraarterial," said Dr. Bindal hesitantly. "The evidence for this is not very clear. The effects would be temporary, and not without some risks, but it may be her only chance for a meaningful recovery."

"Thank you, Dr. Bindal—thank you." John had high hopes for the new treatment plan.

Dr. Bindal spoke to the radiologist and worked out a treatment protocol for the papaverine injection into Stephanie's brain vessels that would dilate the vessels and could counter the effects of vasospasm.

The radiologist ordered a CT scan to ensure Stephanie was not having an actual stroke.

He then performed an angiogram and confirmed severe vasospasm and near occlusion of the carotid artery on the left side, consistent with right sided weakness. The papaverine injection treatment was implemented, and Stephanie's right-sided weakness improved immediately and quite significantly back to normal.

John was ecstatic. His faith in Stephanie's recovery was renewed. He prayed she would continue to do well and that no more treatments would be needed for her vasospasm.

Postoperative Day #5

John walked back into Stephanie's hospital room the next morning after grabbing a cup of coffee from the nurse's station. She had done extremely well overnight. A nurse, dressed in maroon colored scrubs, walked into the room while doing her regular patient rounds to check on Stephanie's status. She stood beside Stephanie's hospital bed.

"If she continues to do well, the doctor said she can be extubated soon," said the nurse. "The doctor is pleased with Stephanie's response to the papaverine treatment. He will be coming shortly to check on Stephanie as well." She decreased Stephanie's sedation medications so that the doctor would be able to do a brief examination when he arrived.

"Can you raise your arms for me Stephanie?" called out the nurse in a loud voice. Stephanie responded by opening her eyes and lifting both arms slowly. She held her arms outstretched with her palms facing upwards for a few moments, when suddenly her right arm began to drift down. Her eyes closed, and she became lethargic. The nurse panicked, and she paged the doctor immediately.

Dr. Bindal was in the middle of patient rounds when he received a page calling him to Stephanie's room for an emergency. His heart sank and he ran quickly to her hospital room. Two nurses were in the room, examining the patient, while John stood in the corner sobbing. Dr. Bindal repeated Stephanie's exam, confirming her right-sided weakness.

"Please do something to help her, Dr. Bindal," begged John. His eyes were sunken. Dr. Bindal shook his head.

"I'm sorry John. As I told you yesterday, this was a last attempt to help Stephanie. She is maxed out on all the possible treatments. I fear she may be suffering serious neurologic damage," said Dr. Bindal.

John stood limp, appearing helpless. All his hopes had been shattered. He wiped the tears from his eyes, looked at Stephanie, then looked back at the doctor.

"Will you pray for her with me?" he asked. Dr. Bindal nodded.

"Of course, John." A hospital chaplain was called into the room. John joined hands with the chaplain and the doctor as the chaplain began a prayer. As the prayer continued, Dr. Bindal was flooded with emotion. He saw the despair in John's face, and he felt compelled to do more for Stephanie.

When the prayer was over, Dr. Bindal decided to convince the radiologist to repeat the papaverine injections once again. John was ecstatic to learn that the doctor had not given up hope completely. The radiologist agreed, albeit hesitantly, to repeat the procedure. He performed another angiogram to confirm the presence of vasospasm as the cause of Stephanie's right-sided weakness, repeated a CT scan to confirm the absence of a true stroke, and then implemented the treatment. Stephanie's weakness improved immediately once again.

Outside the room, Dr. Bindal was finishing his note for Stephanie's chart. The nurse taking care of Stephanie approached him, speaking in a hushed tone.

"Dr. Bindal? I've been wondering about something...why does Stephanie's boyfriend feel so guilty about her condition?"

"Well, I've seen this before in aneurysm rupture patients. If the aneurysm rupture occurs during sex, the partner feels intensely guilty. This guilt is usually not seen in other disease states," he explained.

Postoperative Day #6

The next day, Dr. Bindal was again paged by Stephanie's ICU nurse. He arrived shortly and found the nurse beside Stephanie's bed. John was standing on the opposite side of the bed, his hands clasped tightly over Stephanie's.

"She's having right-sided weakness again, doctor," said the nurse, shaking her head. Dr. Bindal examined the patient, once again confirming her deficits. He turned towards John and opened his mouth to begin speaking. John knew what he had to say. Before could say anything, John interrupted.

"Please, Dr. Bindal. Can't we repeat the papaverine injections?" said John. The doctor shook his head.

"I'm very sorry John. It's dangerous to keep repeating this procedure due to all the risks involved. At some point, we need to give up and let the stroke be complete," said Dr. Bindal. John sobbed violently and repeated his plea.

"Please doctor, please don't give up. Stephanie has to get better. I promise to marry her!" he cried.

"Alright," he said. "We can try the papaverine injections one more time. But we must agree that this will be our last attempt. I will talk with the radiologist and we'll get started right away." The doctor turned to leave the room as John breathed a sigh of relief.

"Thank you, Dr. Bindal. Thank you for not giving up just yet," said John. Dr. Bindal turned and smiled weakly at John, then left the room. He walked towards the radiology suite, where he found the radiologist who had been working with him on Stephanie's treatment.

The radiologist was sitting in the radiology "reading room", a dark, carpeted room filled with cubicles. Within each cubicle was two large, high resolution computer screens which allow the radiologists to view radiographic films with precision. Dr. Bindal found the radiologist seated in one of these cubicles. As he approached, the radiologist looked up from his screen.

"Hi Dr. Lawrence, I wanted to talk to you about our patient Stephanie," said Dr. Bindal.

"Hey Dr. Bindal. Sure, what's up? Is she still doing well?" asked the radiologist.

"Unfortunately, no. She's got right-sided weakness again. I'd like to repeat the intra-arterial papaverine injections one last time." The radiologist furrowed his brow.

"Are you sure? You know the risks involved…We could open the blood vessels too much, and she can have catastrophic bleeding into the brain…" The radiologist trailed off, waiting for an explanation.

"I agree it is risky. I spoke with Stephanie's boyfriend and we discussed it in great detail. He understands that this is the last time we will attempt this."

The radiologist nodded. He performed another angiogram and CT scan on Stephanie as he had done the prior days, then began the papaverine injections. After the treatment was implemented, Dr. Bindal examined Stephanie yet again. She had resolution of her right-sided weakness as she had the last few days. Though he was happy to see her response to the treatment, Dr. Bindal worried she would deteriorate yet again.

That evening, Dr. Bindal stopped by Stephanie's hospital room before leaving the hospital for the day. He found John sitting beside Stephanie's bed, hands clasped tightly, praying silently. John looked up from his prayers as the doctor walked in.

"Hi Dr. Bindal, I wanted to ask you a

question," he said slowly. "All of this neurologic damage that Stephanie is suffering...is she still going to be who she is?" he asked.

"Well, you can lose parts of your brain, but you don't lose who you are. Stephanie may be suffering partial paralysis and having recurring temporary deficits, but she can still be with you. As long as her brainstem is unaffected, she is still who she is," responded the doctor.

John took a moment to think. "What about her memories?"

"You can lose your memories, John, but despite what people think, that does not unmake you from who you were. When you're a child, for example, you have no memories yet, but you are still yourself. An Alzheimer's patient is still who they are. They are still human. Memories are not the only thing that define us," said Dr. Bindal.

John nodded. He looked back at Stephanie and continued his prayers.

Post-operative Day #7

The next morning, Dr. Bindal arrived at the hospital and made his way towards Stephanie's room in the ICU. As he passed the nurse's station in the hallway of her room, he stopped briefly to talk with the night nurse he recognized to be assigned to his patient.

"Good morning Jennifer, how did our patient Stephanie do overnight?" he asked. He watched the nurse's face carefully, worried he would receive bad news.

"She did very well, Dr. Bindal! I had no problems with her. Her neurologic exams overnight were all good. She showed no sign of weakness. I lowered her sedation a few minutes ago so you should be able to examine her," replied the nurse, breaking into a smile. Dr. Bindal breathed a sigh of relief. He walked over to Stephanie's room and knocked on the door, then let himself in. Stephanie's nurse followed behind him.

Stephanie was lying still in the hospital bed. Her head was propped up slightly, and the tube was still in her throat, helping her breathe. John was sleeping on the small pull-out couch in the corner of the room near the windows. The room overlooked the city, and as the sun rose in the distance, a soft light poured in. The handle of the door clicked as it opened, and John looked up from underneath the blankets covering him.

"Hi John, how was Stephanie overnight?" asked the doctor. John sat up on the couch and rubbed his eyes.

"She did well, I think, Dr. Bindal." he replied. Dr. Bindal nodded and examined Stephanie for himself. He asked her to open her eyes and squeeze his fingers with her hands. She was still somewhat sedated, but she was able to follow his commands without problems.

"She looks good, John. We'll continue to watch her closely," said the doctor. He left Stephanie's room to continue his daily work, hopeful that Stephanie was on the path to recovery.

The ICU team continued to watch Stephanie's neurologic status throughout the day. Remarkably, she did not develop any weakness. Day by day, Stephanie's conditioned continued to stabilize, and after two weeks in the ICU, she was stable enough to be transferred to the regular floor. She had survived her bout of vasospasm without significant neurologic stroke. On the floor, she showed continued dramatic improvement of her condition. She was finally discharged to rehabilitation so that she could regain her strength and coordination.

CHAPTER SEVEN

3 Months Later

It was a busy clinic afternoon. Dr. Bindal exited a patient room and was about to turn around to walk back to his office when a lovely young woman entered. She walked towards him, held out her right hand, and spoke. "Thank you, Dr. Bindal, for saving my life."

The doctor had difficulty recognizing this lady, until behind her walked in a tall man with short, dark hair, whom Dr. Bindal immediately recognized as John. He looked back at the young lady and realized she must be Stephanie. Her neurologic condition had returned to normal, and even as a neurosurgeon, it was difficult to perceive that she had suffered any bleeding in her brain.

Stephanie held out her left hand and showed the doctor a small diamond ring that was on her ring finger. John smiled and said, "Guess what Dr. Bindal, we're getting married!"

PART III
APPOINTMENT WITH DEATH

CHAPTER ONE

Jimmy opened the door of his delivery truck and stepped out. As his feet hit the asphalt floor, he felt a sudden loss of balance. The hot, East Texas sun glared down at him as he grabbed the edge of his truck for a moment, regaining his coordination. His legs felt stiff, but he pushed forward and went to the back of his truck to find the package that needed to be delivered to this address. Sorting through the brown cardboard boxes, he found the correct package and made his way up the driveway of the small business in front of him. He walked through the glass doors and approached the young man dressed in a gray suit at the front desk.

"Good afternoon, I have a package to deliver," he said slowly. His tongue felt heavy in his mouth, and the words came out slurred. The man at the desk frowned a little.

"Are you okay, sir?" he replied. The delivery

man sounded drunk.

"I'm sorry, what?" asked Jimmy. He turned his head to the left, hoping he would hear the words better. The hearing in his right ear had slowly deteriorated over the last year.

"Are you okay?" repeated the man. Jimmy nodded.

"Please sign here," he said, again slowly and carefully. He tried his best to make the words sound clear. The young man signed the form, and Jimmy made his way to the glass doors again. He got back in his truck and continued on his delivery route. With each passing day, Jimmy was having greater difficulty carrying out his work responsibilities. He worried he might have to quit his work if things kept getting worse.

Later in the evening, Jimmy arrived at home. His house was a small, two-bedroom cottage. It was a simple structure, a reflection of Jimmy's simple, honest living. As the door opened, his wife, Clara, called out to him.

"Is that you, Jimmy?" she called. Her loud voice boomed through the home. She appeared in the entryway. "Come sit down. How was work today?"

Jimmy stepped forward into the living area, passing by the large decorative sign on the wall reading "I can do all things through God who strengthens me". He sat on the couch, stretching his legs. Clara watched each step he took carefully, then sat beside him, looking at him keenly. "Did you have any problems at work today, honey?" she asked.

"It wasn't terrible. My legs are feeling a little stiff." Jimmy's words were slurred still.

"What about your ear?" she asked.

He shrugged. "It's the same."

"Did you lose your balance at all?"

"I felt unbalanced getting out of the car and walking a little," he replied meekly. Clara threw her arms in the air.

"That's it!" she yelled, her voice loud again. "You have to take time off from work. You cannot continue your work this way. Your voice is slurred, you're losing your balance...you could fall! You aren't a twenty-something year old man anymore. You're forty-five years old. Tomorrow you will call your boss and tell them you need time off to take care of your health. We have an appointment to see the neurosurgeon next week anyways," she said firmly. "I'm really worried about you, Jimmy. I'm watching you get worse day by day. And your mother agrees, you know."

Jimmy had been married to Clara for twenty years now, and he knew better than to argue with her. He nodded his head and accepted his wife's statement. He loved her dearly, and he knew that she had his best interest in mind.

"Yes, dear," he responded. He sighed, hoping his problems would soon go away. Last week, Jimmy had gone to see his family physician, Dr. Piper, for the worsening symptoms he had been having.

"I want to get an MRI scan of your head, Jimmy," Dr. Piper had said. When the radiology report came in, Dr. Piper asked Jimmy and his wife to return to her clinic to discuss the results.

"Your MRI scan shows a large acoustic neuroma, which is a benign tumor of the nerve sheath cells. It is benign, but the tumor is very large. As a result, it is causing significant brainstem compression on the right side. It has blocked the normal flow of cerebrospinal fluid, or CSF, out of your brain, resulting in hydrocephalus, or increased pressure of spinal fluid in the brain."

Jimmy and Clara were shocked by the news. Dr. Piper recommended that Jimmy see a neurosurgeon named Dr. Ajay Bindal in Houston for further treatment of his condition. They scheduled an appointment quickly, and when the time came, they traveled to Houston to see the doctor.

Dr. Bindal was on call for the neurosurgery service. He was paged to see a young patient, a boy who was 17-years-old, who was brought into the trauma bay by helicopter after being involved in a motor vehicle accident. The boy arrived and the trauma personnel swarmed him, only to find that he had fixed, dilated pupils. He was still, not moving any limbs. He looked brain-dead.

Dr. Bindal arrived and spoke with the trauma

surgeons in charge. "Did he get any paralytics?" he asked, trying to determine reasons why the boy may be the way he is.

"No, he didn't. The paramedics didn't say anything about that," responded the trauma surgeon, removing his gloves and gown. He began to leave the room—the situation appeared hopeless. "It looks like we can extubate him and let him go," he said. "We just called you to get the formal assessment." The trauma nurses and staff all exited the room, leaving only the neurosurgeon with the boy.

Though it seemed the trauma surgeon was right, there was something unusual about the case that Dr. Bindal could not let go. The respiratory therapist entered and went to the head of the bed. She placed her hands in position on the tube in the boy's throat, about to remove it, when Dr. Bindal stopped her. "Wait! Don't extubate him yet."

The respiratory therapist complied. Dr. Bindal left the room to find the trauma surgeon, who was sitting in the center of the trauma bay at a computer. "I want to wait to extubate him. Let's give him some time before we declare him dead," he said.

The trauma surgeon shrugged. "He's definitely dead. But sure, why not? I'll just get the paperwork started." He turned back to his computer, typing into the patient's medical chart. Dr. Bindal sat beside him, completing paperwork of his own.

Ten minutes later, they heard the sound of someone coughing emanating from the boy's room.

The trauma surgeon looked up in disbelief, and Dr. Bindal rushed into the room. The nurses and staff jumped from their seats and rushed to follow him in.

The boy was awake. His eyes were open. He was trying to sit up, moving his arms and legs, like a zombie returning from death. Dr. Bindal looked at the trauma surgeon, who turned away in shame. Had they disconnected the boy's breathing tube, he would have died, and no one would have known that he wasn't dead. They later determined that the paramedics had given the boy long-acting paralytics in the helicopter because he was difficult to control and keep calm on their flight to the hospital. They had failed to mention that on arrival.

Shaking his head, Dr. Bindal thought to himself *"One should never rush death."*

CHAPTER TWO

Dr. Bindal knocked on the exam room door. "Come in!" called a loud female voice from inside. He stepped into the room and saw a middle-aged man seated on the exam table and a woman seated on a chair next to him. The woman had her arms crossed, and despite appearing anxious, her presence filled the room. Dr. Bindal walked towards the man on the table and extended his hand.

"Hello, I'm Dr. Bindal. What can I do for you today?" he asked. The man on the exam table opened his mouth to speak, but before he could say anything, the woman spoke.

"Hi Dr. Bindal, I'm Jimmy's wife, Clara. We are here to talk to you about the brain tumor that our family doctor found on Jimmy's MRI," she said. She handed the doctor a disc with the images saved. Dr. Bindal took the disc and loaded it into the computer. He turned back to Jimmy as the images were loading and asked, "Can you tell me more about the symptoms you have been having?"

"Well, I started to notice headaches and problems hearing in my right year," began Jimmy. Dr. Bindal immediately noticed the slurring of his speech.

"How long ago was this?" he asked.

Clara interjected. "A year ago," she said quickly. Jimmy continued his story.

"Yes, it was about a year ago. But I have been having more problems recently. About two months ago, I started having trouble with balance. I feel I walk as if I'm drunk...and I have trouble getting out of chairs and going up stairs."

Clara spoke again. "The balance problems have gotten much worse in the last three weeks, doctor." Dr. Bindal nodded.

Jimmy continued. "I also feel like the right side of my face is numb. And my speech is weird, like I'm drunk or something," he said. "I had to take off from work a few days ago because it's gotten so bad. I have trouble getting in and out of the car...I'm a delivery man. My legs feel very stiff and my coordination is all out of whack."

Clara nodded fervently with each of Jimmy's words. She turned to the doctor. "I'm terrified, doctor. It's been terrible watching him get so much worse so quickly." She sat forward in her chair. "I know he has a brain tumor, doctor. I looked online and read about it a little. Please, doctor, I can't lose my Jimmy. He's all I got. Please tell me you can do something for him!"

Dr. Bindal looked back at the computer to check on the status of the loading disc. The images had finally loaded, and he began scrolling through them. Jimmy's problem was plainly evident. The large acoustic neuroma on the right side of his head was compressing the brainstem and causing hydrocephalus.

"I agree with the diagnosis," said Dr. Bindal, looking up from the computer screen. He picked up a replica of the human skull sitting on the table beside him, using it to help him explain the diagnosis. "Based on the images, it looks like you have an acoustic neuroma, which is a tumor that arises from the hearing and balance nerve. This is a slow-growing tumor. However, given its large size, the tumor is very dangerous. Left untreated, this tumor will take your life," he said.

He paused for a moment, letting his words sink in. Jimmy and his wife appeared in shock, terrified by the doctor's words. Tears appeared in Clara's eyes.

"The tumor is quite large," he repeated. "I recommend it be resected in two stages. We would debulk the tumor in the first stage, allowing the brainstem to recover to a more normal position. About a month or two later, for the second stage, we would dissect the tumor off the nerves and the brainstem very carefully using microdissection and nerve monitoring. The tumor is compressing multiple cranial nerves right now, including the fifth, seventh, eighth, ninth, and tenth nerve. All of these nerves will need to be preserved as the tumor is resected. I am recommending the surgery be done in two stages because of risk of brain swelling, plus both operations will be very long. Are you following me so far?" he asked.

Jimmy and Clara nodded. Dr. Bindal continued. "There is a significant risk of major stroke or vegetative state associated with surgery, but this is your best chance to preserve neurologic function and have recovery. Since you are in town now, we can proceed with the surgery within the week, if you would like. I'll need you to see the Ear Nose and Throat (ENT) surgeon who specializes in neuro-otology before the surgery as well. He will be assisting with this procedure since the tumor is involving the hearing nerve. We do many of these tumors together."

Jimmy looked at his wife. She had tears in her eyes and was unusually quiet. He could tell she was terrified about the future. He took her hands in his own.

"Everything will be alright, honey, I promise. We have to have trust in God and in the doctors," he said gently. He turned to the doctor. "I would like to get the surgery done." Clara agreed, and they began the process of preparing for the operation.

Later that day, as Dr. Bindal entered the hospital to make rounds on his patients, he walked past a gentleman sitting in a wheelchair alone and unattended who had suffered head injury. He could see a dip in the curvature of the man's head where a piece of skull was likely missing. The patient was unkempt, smelling of urine. His ability to think was clearly crippled. He had no well-wishers nor any family. Dr. Bindal wondered if the man was comfortable, if he was happy. He wondered at the humanity left in this patient. He wondered if he still had a soul.

As a doctor, when you deal with so much death, you come to appreciate life. Every day that a man can open his eyes and enjoy life is a gift. The pager beeped ferociously. Dr. Bindal was called to the trauma bay for two patients, both involved in a high-speed motor vehicle crash on the freeway. One patient, a 19-year-old man, had bilateral hemispheric contusions in his brain. His brain was swollen, and he had loss of his basal cisterns. He came to the trauma bay intubated. The other patient, a 35-year-old female, arrived intubated as well. She had severe brain injury, and she had lost all brainstem reflexes.

Dr. Bindal confirmed the absence of all brainstem reflexes in the female patient. He decided to hold her for an observation period of six hours to confirm brain death. Meanwhile, the young man's neurologic status was deteriorating quickly. Dr. Bindal began treatment of the young man with hyperventilation, mannitol, and CSF drainage by placing a drain in his head. His intracranial pressure continued to rise, and though brainstem findings were still intact, his pupils were beginning to look fixed and dilated. Dr. Bindal finally decided to put the patient into a barbiturate coma.

The barbiturate coma is the ultimate in anesthesia, bringing patients as close to death as possible. Used as a treatment for rising intracranial pressures, it consists of high dose barbiturate therapy which is given as a last resort measure after all other treatments have failed. Mimicking an opioid overdose, it suppresses all brain function, including brainstem reflexes. The heartbeat slows to near dangerous levels, sometimes requiring medications to help pump the heart faster. The immune system stops working, making patients susceptible to pneumonias and other infections. The gut ceases to digest, resulting in a paralytic ileus.

With the young man in a barbiturate coma, and the other in observation of brain death, a nurse remarked on the similarity between the two patients.

"They both have the same physical exam...how is she dead, but he isn't?" she asked.

"As long as a patient is getting drugs that suppress neurologic function, you can't declare them to be dead, even if they may appear to be," he answered.

A transplant surgeon entered the trauma bay and approached Dr. Bindal. "I heard you have a patient who is brain dead? She's listed as an organ donor. I'd like to take her now," he said roughly.

"No, she's not dead until I declare her so. We have to observe her for six hours first," said Dr. Bindal.

"What's going to change in six hours? We have patients waiting for these organs!" replied the transplant surgeon.

"No... we have to wait six hours. You don't want to end up in a newspaper with the claim that you are stealing organs from people before they are dead. Trust me." The trauma surgeon agreed to wait, and six hours later, he took the woman to the operating room to harvest her organs.

CHAPTER THREE

The day of Jimmy's operation had arrived. As the doctor had mentioned in the clinic visit, he would perform the first stage of the operation today, followed by the second stage later. Jimmy arrived with his wife and mother at the hospital in Houston early in the morning. They spent the last week completing all the preoperative work-up needed to be ready for today.

Once the operating room was meticulously prepared by the nurses, Jimmy was ready to be taken back from the preoperative holding area. The nurse grabbed the handles on his bed and unlocked his gurney, preparing to wheel him away. Clara bent down and kissed Jimmy, her eyes swollen with tears. His mother took his hands and kissed him on the forehead. Jimmy looked at both of them and reassured them. "Everything will be alright," he said. "Have trust in God and in Dr. Bindal's hands." The nurse pushed his bed out of the door towards the operating room.

In the operating room, the anesthesiologist anesthetized Jimmy and intubated him, then placed him on his side in the lateral oblique position. Dr. Bindal placed his head in the Mayfield head holder and shaved and cleaned the back of his head. He had spent the morning mentally preparing for the surgery. He knew that in order to perform the surgery, he would need to retract on Jimmy's brain which would increase the pressure in his head even further, potentially causing him to herniate and die. To avoid this problem, he decided to place a drain just above the back of Jimmy's ear to allow fluid to drain, keeping the pressure in Jimmy's brain normal.

The nurses placed monitoring leads on Jimmy to allow neurophysiologic monitoring during the procedure. Although this was more important for the second procedure that was planned, Dr. Bindal decided it was worth monitoring the brainstem during this stage of the operation as well.

Dr. Bindal scrubbed his hands and arms in the large sinks outside the operating room, then returned and dressed in the gown, ready for the procedure. He began by drilling a hole in Jimmy's skull, then placed a catheter to drain fluid. With the drain in place, he was ready to begin opening the skull to debulk the tumor.

Dr. Bindal created an opening in Jimmy's skull behind the right ear and back of the skull that was large enough to allow proper debulking of the tumor and would also give the brain room to expand in case of intraoperative brain swelling. As he cut through the protective layers covering the brain, the tumor came into view. It was a gray color, easily differentiated from the healthy pink tissue making up the normal brain. The tumor was the size of a fist, taking up a substantial portion of the posterior fossa, which is the space in the skull near the brainstem and cerebellum.

Tha dump...tha dump...tha dump

Beep beep...beep beep...beep beep

Tick tock...tick tock...tick tock

The symphony of the operating room resonated through the air loudly.

Slowly, Dr. Bindal resected as much of the tumor he thought was safely possible before getting to the delicate part of dealing with the brainstem and nerves. Near the end of the resection process, Dr. McAlister, the ENT doctor, entered the operating room to check on the progress. He was an older surgeon with an expertise in neuro-otology. His role in the operation was mostly reserved for the second stage, during which they would be working close to the nerve responsible for hearing.

"Hey Ajay, how is everything?" he asked behind his mask, peering over the surgical field from behind Dr. Bindal, making sure not to touch anything around him.

"Hey Will. Everything is going well so far," replied Dr. Bindal. "I'm just about to finish up. I haven't had any problems so far."

"I just wanted to come in and check on how

things were going so far." He continued to observe the procedure for a few minutes, then left the OR.

Dr. Bindal finished as much of the resection as he wanted done that day, then closed the opening in Jimmy's skull. He cleaned the blood off Jimmy's head and applied a bandage. The nurses removed the monitoring leads and placed warm blankets on Jimmy. The anesthesiologist left the tube in Jimmy's throat due to concerns about his brainstem and vocal cord function, as well as post-operative swelling. They pushed Jimmy's gurney through the large doors of the operating room out into the hallway towards the recovery room, with Dr. Bindal following close behind.

In the recovery room, Jimmy showed improvement. Once he was assured that Jimmy was secure, Dr. Bindal went to the family waiting area to talk with Clara and her mother-in-law.

Clara and her mother-in-law were waiting anxiously for Dr. Bindal to enter the waiting room. When he entered, they stood quickly and walked to him, earnestly searching his face for clues as to what had happened. Dr. Bindal smiled. "Everything went well with Jimmy today. There were no complications during the procedure," he said.

"Thank the Lord!" exclaimed the two women, smiling broadly. They were ecstatic with the results.

"We will watch Jimmy in the recovery room for a short while. Once he's ready, we will take the tube out of his throat and move him to the ICU.

Now, I have to warn you, tonight is the most critical time for Jimmy. There is a risk of postoperative bleeding and brain swelling. We will watch him closely in the ICU for any changes in his condition," said the doctor. He saw the worry in Clara's face as he spoke. Although the surgery had gone as planned, he felt it was important to warn patients of any possible dangers or challenges that could occur in the future.

Later in the recovery room, the anesthesiologist removed the tube from Jimmy's throat and he was taken to the ICU. Jimmy was awake and able to talk now. His neurologic status had returned to the baseline deficits he had prior to surgery. Clara and her mother-in-law arrived in the ICU room and stood by Jimmy's side. Jimmy looked up at the two most important women in his life, and smiled slowly.

"See, what did I tell you?" said Jimmy. He moved his hand towards hers. "Everything is alright."

They clasped their hands tightly together, and Clara prayed for Jimmy's speedy and complete recovery. Dr. Bindal stood in the room and watched this emotional display of affection. The love that Clara displayed struck his heart.

"*Jimmy is a lucky man,*" he thought to himself. "*I hope Jimmy does well, for Clara's sake.*"

Dr. Bindal went home late that day, tired from the day's long surgery. As soon as he arrived home, he ate dinner with his wife and four children, then went to his bedroom to sleep. He hoped to get a good night's rest before work the next day. As he lay down to sleep, the image of Clara holding Jimmy's hands and praying came in his mind. The image slowly melted away as he fell into a deep sleep.

CHAPTER FOUR

2 Years Previously

It was late afternoon on a summer day. A surgery at the hospital was canceled at the last minute, and Dr. Bindal arrived home early that day. Soon after arriving, he received frantic phone calls from the son of a close family friend, Monica. Earlier that day, Monica had collapsed at home and had suffered anoxic brain injury and subsequent brain swelling. Dr. Bindal rushed to the hospital with his wife, and arrived in the family waiting area where Monica's son and husband were sitting. The hospital was one in which Dr. Bindal did not normally practice, so it was one of the few moments in his life when he witnessed patient care from the family's point of view. The local neurosurgeon had stabilized Monica and was managing her care.

Dr. Bindal and his wife entered the family waiting area. Monica's family was sobbing. Seeing Dr.

Bindal, they stood to greet him.

"We're so glad you're here, Ajay. Can you please see her?" asked Monica's son. Dr. Bindal went into Monica's room. It was difficult to see her in the hospital bed, tube down her throat, vulnerable. He remembered her to be an active woman, known well in society for her personable character. She was some years younger than his own mother—too young to be in this state. He went to her bedside and looked at her. He was there as a friend, so he did nothing more.

He returned to the family waiting area, when Monica's doctor arrived. Dr. Bindal immediately recognized the doctor as an internal medicine specialist, Dr. Nelly, that he knew well and had worked with in the past. Dr. Nelly shook hands with Dr. Bindal fervently.

"Dr. Bindal, it's so good to see you! Are you going to be taking care of Monica?" he asked.

"Hi Dr. Nelly. No, I'm just here as family. I don't practice at this hospital," he said.

"Well, Monica has suffered serious damage to her brain. She's lost some brainstem reflexes, but not all. The situation is very serious," replied Dr. Nelly gravely.

"Ajay, you have to take care of her, please," said Monica's son. "I really want you to manage her care."

"Your neurosurgeon is good and has given you the right advice. Why do you need me to take over her care?" asked Dr. Bindal.

"Maybe his advice is right, but you give us hope."

Dr. Nelly nodded in agreement. "Yes, Dr. Bindal, I've worked many times with you before. I insist you take over Monica's management."

"Well, I can't really do this because I don't practice at this hospital. I don't have access to the computer system...I can't—" Dr. Nelly interrupted, waving his hands in the air.

"We'll take care of all that." Dr. Nelly assured Dr. Bindal that he would take care of any necessary paperwork. And so, somewhat unwillingly, Dr. Bindal took over Monica's care.

He examined Monica and found that she had some brainstem reflexes left, but she was definitely severely brain injured. He initiated treatments for brain swelling. Over the course of observation for a few days, she showed some improvement. She had some response on pinching of her extremities, but she remained severely impaired. Dr. Bindal felt it was important to be truthful with his close friends.

"Unfortunately, she appears to have severe brain injury. It may be better to let her go because if she recovers, she would recover in a severely brain injured state," he said to Monica's husband and son. They refused, unwilling to let her go. They saw through their doctor friend a ray of hope. Dr. Bindal realized that they likely needed a little time to accept Monica's fate.

They carried on in this way for a week. Dr. Bindal would examine her every day. Every time, the room would fill with family members, all looking intensely at the doctor, looking for a glimmer of hope. Despite that, he never failed in his responsibility to tell them the truth. He allowed them to hold on to their optimism, hoping they would eventually come to the realization of what was the right thing to do. After several days of improvement, she began to show no change. Dr. Bindal warned them that she would eventually deteriorate to brain death.

"What if she's brain dead? Can't we just keep her alive on the ventilator?" asked Monica's son.

"No, you can't, because the body will die eventually. The only way a patient can live indefinitely on a ventilator is if they are not truly brain dead," he explained.

"But her heart would still be beating, and she would still be breathing. She would still be alive, right?"

Dr. Bindal shook his head. "The body cannot live without the brain. She may not be fully brain dead yet, but she will be due to brain swelling. Brain swelling causes brain herniation and all the brainstem neurons die. At that point, she will be declared dead—brain dead. Even if not declared brain dead, her heart and body will fail and she cannot be sustained by machines."

The next day, while eating dinner at a

restaurant, Dr. Bindal received an emergency call regarding Monica. She had a second episode of deterioration, and she had herniated her brain. He arrived at the hospital shortly, and the family was sobbing. It was clear to Dr. Bindal that they had finally come to accept her death. He entered her room to examine her.

She was still, unresponsive to pinching and any other noxious stimuli. He checked her eyes, and found her pupils fixed, unresponsive to light. He touched the corneas of her eyes with cotton, and she did not blink. He poured cold water into her ears, and again, no response. He moved the tube in her throat, attempting to elicit a gag response from the tissue deep her in throat. Finally, he disconnected the ventilator and watched her for spontaneous respirations, which is the final step in the evaluation of brain death. She had lost all brainstem reflexes, and she was declared dead. Though he was not able to save her life, her family thanked him for giving them hope.

At 2 o'clock in the morning, the night nurse taking care of Jimmy in the ICU went quietly into his room to examine him once again. She was instructed to perform neurologic exams on her patient every hour.

The nurse approached Jimmy's bed and nudged him gently to wake him up.

"Hi Mr. Jimmy, can you wake up for me?" she

asked. He didn't respond at first. She tapped his hand, calling his name louder this time.

"Mr. Jimmy, can you please wake up?" Jimmy still had no answer. She became worried, and began to tap his hand and shoulder aggressively, attempting to get a response out of him. He lay still in the bed, eyes closed, with no movement.

The nurse was now extremely concerned. She pinched Jimmy's fingers and toes with as much strength as she could muster. When he remained unresponsive, she pressed firmly down on his chest with her hands, increasing the stimulation in the hopes of eliciting a response. She checked his pupils with her pen light—they were fixed and dilated. The heart monitor on the side of the bed remained normal. She grabbed a tongue depressor and shoved it down Jimmy's throat, hoping to elicit his gag reflex by irritating the tissues deep in his throat. He continued to be unresponsive. She called two more nurses into the room to confirm her findings.

Jimmy's wife and mother were awakened by this point by the commotion. Clara stood and began to panic as she watched the nurse attempt to wake Jimmy.

"What's happening? Why isn't he waking up?" she asked repetitively to the nurse. The nurse ignored Clara, unable to provide an answer at this time. She moved quickly to the phone and paged the anesthesiologist on call so that Jimmy could be intubated once again. The other two nurses continued to attempt to stimulate Jimmy.

The anesthesiologist arrived in a few moments, and he immediately moved to the head of Jimmy's bed. Clara and her mother-in-law continued to panic. They could tell something was wrong.

"Can we move the family to a waiting room please?" demanded the anesthesiologist, as he placed a tube in Jimmy's throat to help him breathe. A nurse moved Clara and her mother-in-law out of the room, reassuring them that she would update them with answers as soon as they spoke with the doctor. Then, she went to a telephone and dialed the number for the neurosurgeon who was in charge of Jimmy's care.

"Hi, Dr. Bindal? I'm calling about your patient Jimmy. He's looking brain-dead."

Dr. Bindal immediately sprung from his bed. His heart rate and blood pressure shot up. It was his worst nightmare—getting a call from an ICU nurse that a formerly awake patient appears "brain-dead". When a patient loses their brainstem reflexes, recovery from intervention is deemed essentially impossible.

"What? Okay—get an emergency CT head scan now. I'll be there ASAP. Also, give mannitol and hyperventilate," he said quickly. He put on his scrubs and rushed to the hospital. When he arrived at the hospital, he ran straight to Jimmy's room. His room was dark, and the staff was solemn. The anesthesiologist was watching Jimmy's respiration on the ventilator.

"The patient didn't receive any paralytics, correct?" asked Dr. Bindal. The anesthesiologist confirmed this. Dr. Bindal examined the patient, repeating the maneuvers that the nurses had performed. He opened Jimmy's emergency CT scan on the computer. The CT scan did not show any bleeding. However, there was significant swelling in the back of the brain around the tumor. The swelling was of sufficient degree to press against the brainstem and cause Jimmy to lose all his brainstem reflexes and appear "brain-dead".

Dr. Bindal was shocked to see such significant swelling and loss of neurologic function. The situation appeared hopeless. A thousand thoughts entered his mind, all questioning why Jimmy had deteriorated so suddenly.

"The surgery went well... he was awake and talking earlier. Why did this happen?" he thought to himself.

"Dr. Bindal?" A nurse's voice brought him back to reality.

"Dr. Bindal? The patient's wife and mother are waiting to hear from you in the waiting room. I just thought you should know..." she trailed off. Dr. Bindal looked up and sighed. He nodded, and left the room to talk with Clara and her mother-in-law.

Clara and Jimmy's mother were in the waiting room, anxiously waiting to hear from the doctor. As he walked through the doors of the waiting room, Clara's eyes met his, and she immediately perceived the hopeless situation. He saw the dread on Clara's

153

face, and he shook his head sadly.

It struck Clara that Jimmy had died. Before the doctor could say a word, she let out a scream that was so loud, it could pierce the heart of God.

"NOOO!" The sound, loud and shrill, came from the depths of her body. It was the wail of a wife who had lost her husband.

"I'm sorry," said Dr. Bindal. "Jimmy looks like he is brain-dead." Clara moved towards the doctor and grabbed him, her hands firmly on his shoulders.

"You have to do something. You have to save him!" she screamed.

"I'm sorry. I can't save him if he is already dead," he replied.

"Jimmy, you promised me this wouldn't happen! You can't leave me alone! Lord, this can't be. Oh, God, this can't be," wailed Clara. "Dr. Bindal, please save my Jimmy. *Please*, is there any chance you can save my Jimmy?" she sobbed.

"No, Clara. I'm sorry. Jimmy is dead." He shook his head.

"*No*, Dr. Bindal. Please save him. *Please* save my Jimmy." Clara pleaded with the doctor, retaining her firm grip on his shoulders.

Dr. Bindal took a deep breath, paused, and searched within himself for an answer. He had given bad news to patients' families numerous times before, but Clara's actions struck him in a way no one else had.

"Okay, let's rush him to the operating room and see what we can do," he said, after a few moments. Clara let out a sigh of relief, tears still flowing from her eyes.

"I know you can do it, Dr. Bindal. I have faith in you. God will work his miracles through your hands," she said, taking his hands in hers.

Despite Clara's firm belief in Jimmy's ability to recover, Dr. Bindal felt it was highly unlikely he would make a recovery. Jimmy had now been in a state of death for at least half an hour. It would be an absolute miracle if he was able to come back to life, and even if he lived, meaningful neurologic recovery was unlikely due to the brain damage he had likely suffered.

Dr. Bindal returned to Jimmy's room quickly. The nurses looked at him intently. "Is he dead, doctor?" asked one of the nurses.

"Well, I haven't tested his respiration because he's on the ventilator, so he doesn't meet criteria for brain death."

"Should we take him off the ventilator then?"

"No. I decided to take him back to the operating room. Since we aren't interested in determining brain death, we won't take him off the ventilator."

"But shouldn't we check first? Make sure he is alive and has a positive apnea test?"

"If we have any intention of trying to save him, we can't turn off the ventilator and deprive him of oxygen for eight to ten minutes to decide whether or not he meets the requirement for brain death. What do you think that would do to brain function, if there is any left?" The nurses nodded in understanding. They began to prepare Jimmy for transport to the operating room.

CHAPTER FIVE

It was 2:30 AM, and Dr. Bindal did not have his usual daytime operating room team. Jimmy was already in the OR on the operating table, and the OR staff were quickly preparing him and the room for the operation. The scrub and circulating nurses put together the tools needed for the operation in the best way they could manage, not knowing Dr. Bindal's preferences since they had never worked with him before.

The operating room was eerily silent to Dr. Bindal's ears.

He cleaned Jimmy's head, then scrubbed in. He re-opened the incision that he had sewn less than twelve hours ago, and opened the dura. The amount of swelling in Jimmy's brain was tremendous. As he opened the dura, Jimmy's brain immediately bulged out of the opening. The only way to make room in Jimmy's skull would be to remove portions of normal brain.

The doctor began the process of decompressing Jimmy's brain. He removed portions of the cerebellum that were swollen, relieving the pressure from the swollen brain tissue until finally the brain looked more calm. By now, it was 3:30 AM, and Dr. Bindal was exhausted. He looked down in the cavity and saw the tumor that he had previously left behind. He looked up at the OR staff, all people he had never worked with before, then looked at the way the room had been set up. There was no microscope. There was no neurophysiologic monitoring. The emergent way in which the room was set up meant none of the high-tech equipment he would typically use to remove tumor from the nerves and brainstem were present.

The operating room was silent. Tired and sleepy, Dr. Bindal couldn't even hear his own heartbeat. As he stared again at the residual brain tumor in the cavity, a power unbeknownst to him compelled him to remove more tumor. *"Maybe I can take some more tumor out,"* he thought to himself. He began to carefully dissect tumor off the nerves and brainstem, working slowly and steadily.

1996—Mayfield Clinic, Cincinnati, Ohio

Dr. Bindal was in the OR, preparing a patient for surgery. It was the resident physician's job to make sure the operating room and patient were ready for the attending physician. The patient had a small tumor called an acoustic neuroma. The attending on the case, Dr. Sheb, was a Middle-Eastern neurosurgeon known for his speed.

Dr. Sheb walked into the OR and approached Dr. Bindal, slapping him on the back. "So, Ajay, how long is this surgery going to take today?"

Dr. Bindal looked up and thought for a moment. "At least a few hours, sir," he responded.

Dr. Sheb shook his head. "Nope. We are going to take this tumor out in forty-five minutes flat, from the beginning to the end. I have to pick up my kids from school in an hour." Dr. Sheb was recently divorced, and as part of his divorce settlement, he had the right to pick his children up from school. He loved his children dearly, and the time he was allotted to spend with them was too precious to give up.

Dr. Bindal raised his eyebrows. Performing the operation in forty-five minutes was impossible— the exposure alone would take that much time.

"Uh...that's impossible sir. Making the opening itself will take…" Dr. Sheb cut in.

"No, in fact, *you* are going to do the surgery, and I will watch. *You* are going to complete this operation in forty-five minutes. It's a matter of technique." Dr. Sheb smiled behind his mask.

They began the operation, and Dr. Sheb taught Dr. Bindal how to use the instruments in new ways to quickly dissect the tissues. When it came time to remove the tumor from the nerves, Dr. Bindal looked up and addressed the nurses.

"Can we get the microscope ready?" he asked. Dr. Sheb put his hand up and stopped them.

"No microscope. We don't need it." Dr. Bindal was shocked again.

"Continue what you were doing," commanded Dr. Sheb. He taught Dr. Bindal how to use special instruments to dissect the tumor from the nerves without the aid of a microscope nor neuromonitoring. Exactly forty-five minutes later, the surgery was complete. Dr. Bindal looked up at the clock with surprise. He couldn't believe the surgery could be done so quickly.

"See, I told you that it could be done," chuckled Dr. Sheb.

It was now 7:30 AM. The sun rose, removing the darkness of the night. The daytime staff poured in and switched out with the night staff, bringing life to the hospital. This included Dr. Bindal's day time nursing team. Dr. Bindal had been working diligently the whole night to remove the residual tumor that he had initially left for the second operation. The music of the operating room was blurred in the distance as he worked in silence in a daze-like manner. He stopped for a moment to stretch his neck, and he peered into the tumor cavity. He found that he could not see any more tumor with his naked eye. Without a microscope, it was difficult to tell how much tumor was left on the nerves.

"Wouldn't it be interesting if I succeeded in removing

the remainder of the tumor without the aid of any high-tech equipment in the middle of the night without my preferred operating room team?' he thought to himself.

The OR doors opened, and Dr. McAlister walked in, tying his mask to his face. With him, the sounds of the operating room came rushing back to Dr. Bindal's mind as he was awoken from his trance.

"What are you doing?" he asked Dr. Bindal, surprised to see him in the operating room. "Are you operating on our acoustic neuroma patient? Do I need to do my part?" He peered into the cavity with Dr. Bindal. The two of them looked carefully, not really seeing any residual tumor.

"No... I'm not going to waste time removing tumor off the nerves of a patient who may be dead," responded Dr. Bindal.

"It looks like you don't really need my help anyways. I can't really see any tumor, although we can't be sure without a microscope," said Dr. McAlister.

"If he survives, I'm going to bring him back for a third operation. I'll finish removing any residual tumor then." Dr. Bindal closed the opening in Jimmy's head and finished the surgery. Finally, they moved Jimmy to the recovery room once again. Clara and Jimmy's mother were brought to the recovery room so that they could see Jimmy. The two ladies were anxious to see the results of the surgery. Their eyes were red from crying all night long.

Dr. Bindal stood at the foot of Jimmy's bed,

watching him intently. As the sedation wore off, he called Jimmy's name in a loud, clear voice.

"Jimmy? Jimmy! Can you hear me Jimmy!" he repeated loudly. There was no movement. He tried again, this time louder, while simultaneously tapping Jimmy's hand.

"Jimmy! Open your eyes for me!" He was nearly shouting now. There was still no movement. Dr. Bindal shook his head and shrugged his shoulders.

"It was a long shot, really. I'm afraid Jimmy might be gone," he said quietly. He turned his back on Jimmy, when suddenly a nurse called out.

"Wait! I think I see something!" she exclaimed. Dr. Bindal turned quickly and looked at Jimmy's face. By some mysterious power, Jimmy fluttered his eyes open. It was as if he had heard the doctor's fateful words, and in an attempt to prove he was still there, he finally mustered the strength to respond.

Dr. Bindal could not believe his eyes. It was nothing short of a miracle. Clara threw her hands in the air and screamed. Tears flowed from her eyes, and she stood and hugged the doctor tightly.

"Thank you, doctor! You saved my husband!" she cried. Dr. Bindal shook his head with disbelief.

"Actually, Clara, it was *you* who saved your husband."

CHAPTER SIX

"THIS IS THE MAN, FOLKS!" shouted Clara. "Dr. Bindal! Let me give you a big kiss! You saved my husband's life!" She grabbed the doctor in a bear hug, kissing him on the cheek. Clara's voice traveled through the hospital hallways. Other doctors and nurses turned and looked to see the source of the commotion.

The night nurse who had originally found Jimmy in his near-death stage, now working a day shift, saw Dr. Bindal down the hall. She approached him later, once Clara and Jimmy's mother had returned to the room.

"So, Dr. Bindal, I've been meaning to ask you a question..." She trailed off, appearing uncomfortable.

"Yes?"

"Well...was the patient dead? Did you bring

him back to life? Or was he never dead?" she finally blurted.

Dr. Bindal chuckled. "Jimmy lost all of his brainstem reflexes," he started. "The only thing we didn't test was his respiration, which would test the deepest center of his brainstem. It's likely that at the time the surgery was done, a few of his brainstem reticulating cells were still alive, and that is why he survived and is fine today. It just comes to show how much damage the brainstem can actually suffer and then recover. Credit goes to the nursing team that responded so quickly." Dr. Bindal shrugged his shoulders with an expression of uncertainty. Despite all the science that has been discovered over centuries, doctors still cannot explain everything.

Jimmy had been in the ICU for a few days now. His neurologic functions were slowly returning. Clara and Jimmy's mother were ecstatic to see his recovery. After a few weeks in the hospital, Jimmy was ready to be discharged for rehabilitation to help him recover his strength and coordination.

"I'd like to follow Jimmy for a little while," said Dr. Bindal to Clara on the day of his discharge. "In three months, we'll get another scan of his brain so we can see how much tumor is left. At that point, I'll plan a third operation to remove all the remaining tumor." Clara nodded in agreement, understanding that this was still not the end of Jimmy's journey.

---

3 Months Later

After a stint in rehabilitation, Jimmy's neurologic condition recovered to a level better than the first time Dr. Bindal had seen him. He returned to the doctor's office in three months with a MRI scan of his head. He walked into the doctor's office with a strength and coordination that he hadn't felt in a long time. In the exam room, Jimmy handed the doctor the disc of his images. Dr. Bindal loaded the images into the computer and began scrolling through them.

"Let's see what we got here," he said. He looked carefully at each image, squinting at the computer screen. Jimmy and Clara watched the doctor intently as he looked at the images.

"Wow...I can't believe it..." started Dr. Bindal. He broke into a broad smile. "There's no residual tumor..." He trailed off, absolutely bewildered. "*I must have removed it all during that second operation...*" he thought to himself.

"Well Jimmy, it looks like you won't need a third operation after all," finished the doctor. Clara and Jimmy hugged each other tightly.

"Not bad for a dead man, huh Dr. Bindal?" asked Jimmy.

AFTERWORD

Over a decade later, my dad met Archer by chance at a large wedding. His neurologic function remains unchanged, and his tumor fully resected with no recurrence. Stephanie wrote my dad a letter fourteen years later describing her life and marriage to her husband John. Fifteen years later, Jimmy came to my dad's office with Clara. They brought with them a long-term MRI that still showed no recurrent tumor.

Medicine is more than just science. It is an art, and there is a supernatural component to it that no doctor can explain. If Archer, Stephanie, and Jimmy had been treated by the standards of care dictated by committees of medicine, they may all be dead today. They were instead treated in ways that many doctors would suggest were unlikely to work. They defied the predictions of medical science. Their lives today are a reflection of the faith their loved ones had.

What does it mean to have a soul? In a

spiritual sense, the soul is defined by the belief in God and in ourselves. As long as we have the strong desire to live and to interact with our loved ones, we have a soul. Our souls define our humanity. Without it, our lives would be like that of inanimate objects, which exist, then cease to exist.

From the scientific standpoint, the brainstem is the seat of the soul. What is the soul, and who is God? The soul is the patient. God is the whole United States—all the people that make the products that made this medical care possible. God is manifest as the surgeon, in whose hands the summation of medical knowledge works as magic. God is luck or chance. Both God and the soul are indescribable. So, dear father, how can one learn the indescribable in medical school?

Made in the USA
Coppell, TX
22 March 2022